MANGA MATH MYSTERIES

THE RUNAWAY PUPPY

A Mystery with Probability

by Lydia Barriman

illustrated by Becky Grutzik

#8

GRAPHIC UNIVERSE™ • MINNEAPOLIS • NEW YORK

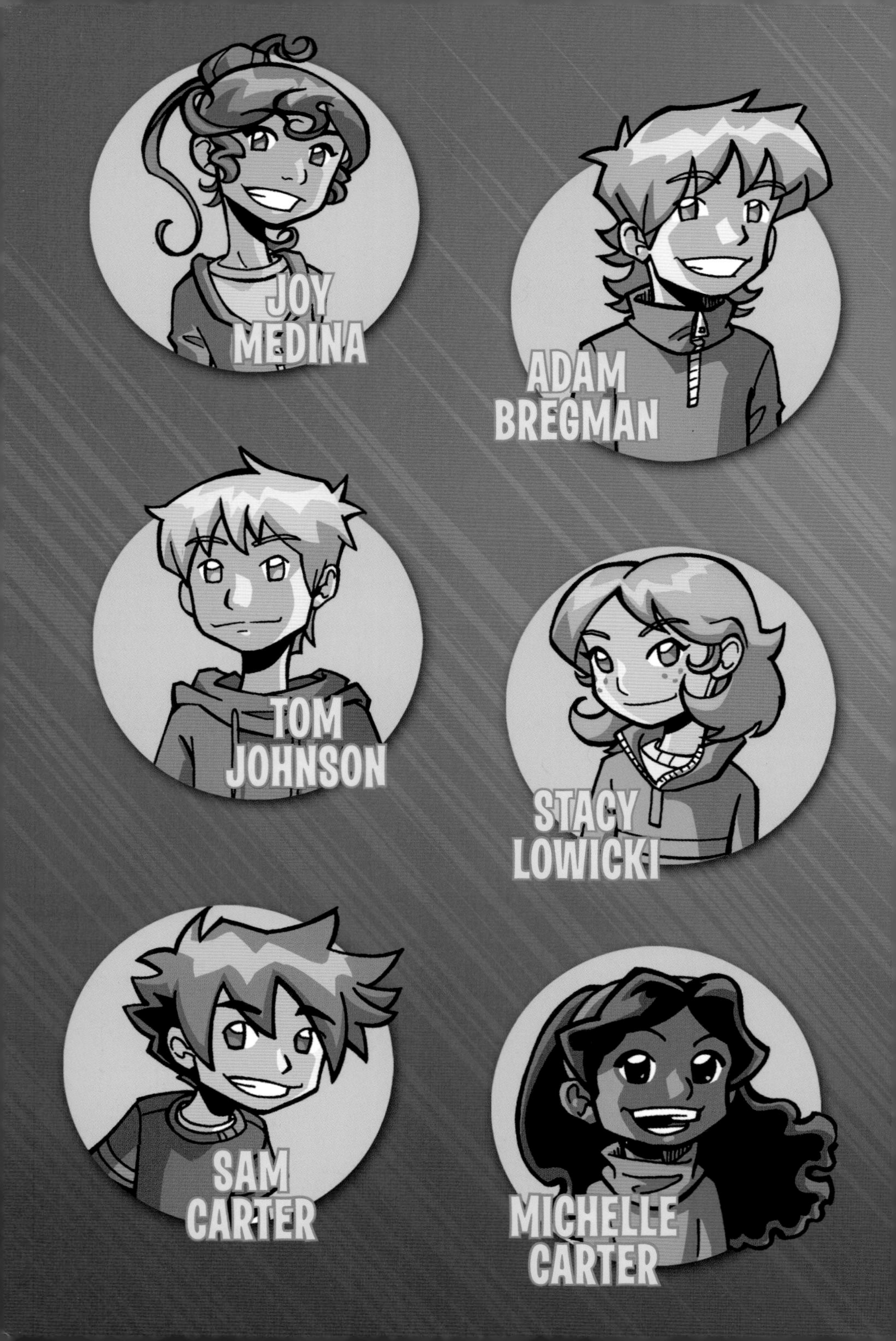
JOY MEDINA
ADAM BREGMAN
TOM JOHNSON
STACY LOWICKI
SAM CARTER
MICHELLE CARTER

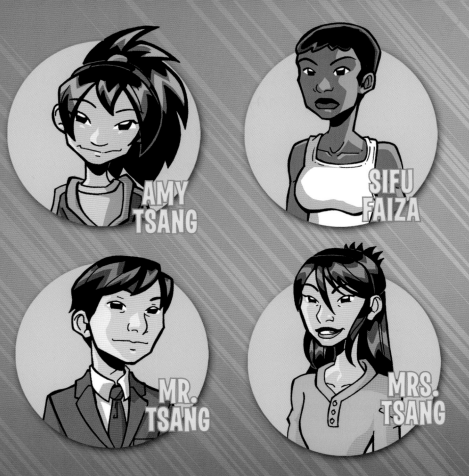

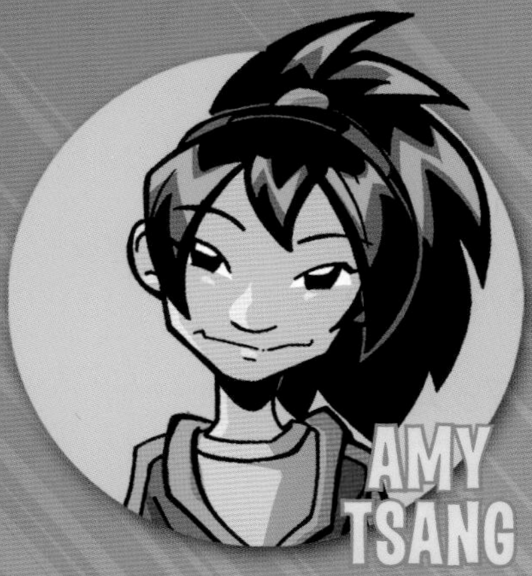
AMY TSANG
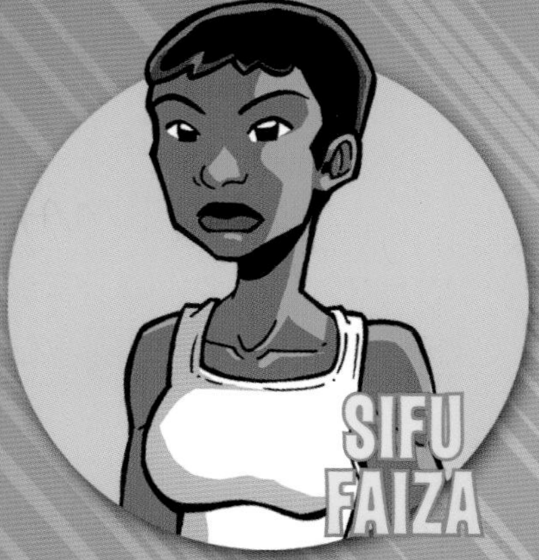
SIFU FAIZA
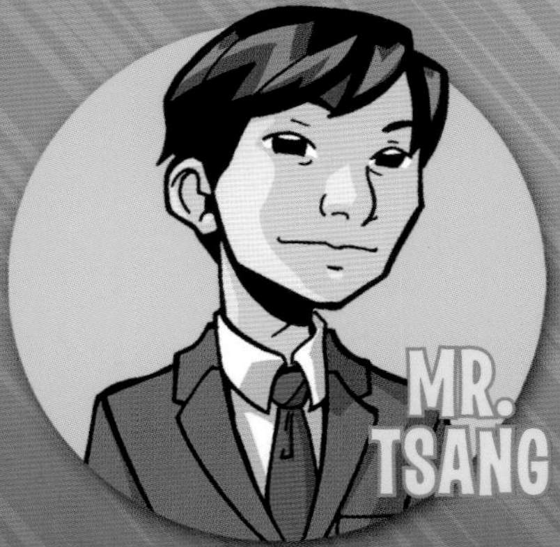
MR. TSANG
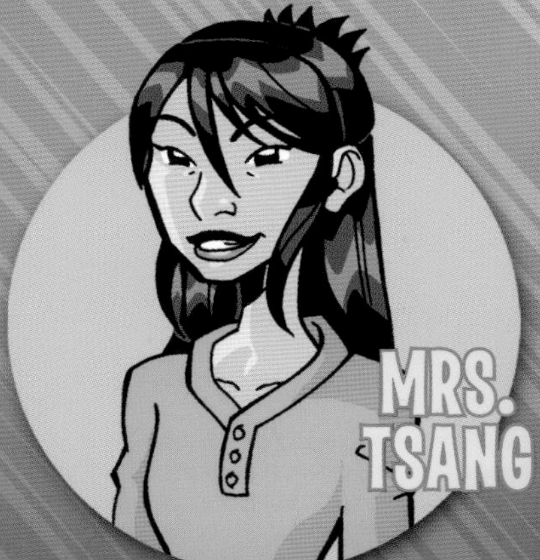
MRS. TSANG

Probability is the chance that something will happen. It's often helpful to know if an outcome is likely or unlikely. Probability uses numbers to help us decide how likely an outcome is. We can think of probability as a fraction, or a part, of the total number of possible outcomes.

When we flip a coin and call heads or tails, we're using probability. The coin has just 2 sides, so the chance of the coin landing on heads is 1 in 2. The probability of it landing on tails is also 1 in 2. We know they are equally likely outcomes. When we roll dice, there are more possible outcomes. A die has 6 sides, so the probability of rolling a certain number is 1 in 6.

Story by Lydia Barriman
Pencils and inks by Becky Grutzik
Coloring by Hi-Fi Design
Lettering by Grace Lu

Graphic Universe™
A division of Lerner Publishing Group, Inc.
241 First Avenue North
Minneapolis, MN 55401 U.S.A.

Website address: www.lernerbooks.com

Library of Congress Cataloging-in-Publication Data

Barriman, Lydia.
     The runaway puppy : a mystery with probability / by Lydia Barriman ; illustrated by Becky Grutzik.
        p. cm. — (Manga math mysteries ; #8)
     Summary: When Amy's puppy runs away, the kung fu students make a bar chart showing places the dog is most familiar with and how often she has visited them in order to determine the probability of where she might be.
     ISBN: 978–0–7613–4910–5 (lib. bdg. : alk. paper)
     1. Graphic novels. [1. Graphic novels. 2. Mystery and detective stories.
3. Mathematics—Fiction. 4. Lost and found possessions—Fiction. 5. Dogs—
Fiction. 6. Animals—Infancy—Fiction. 7. Kung fu—Fiction.] I. Grutzik, Becky, ill.
II. Title.
PZ7.7.B37Run 2011
741.5'973—dc22   2010001432

Manufactured in the United States of America
2 – DP – 7/1/11

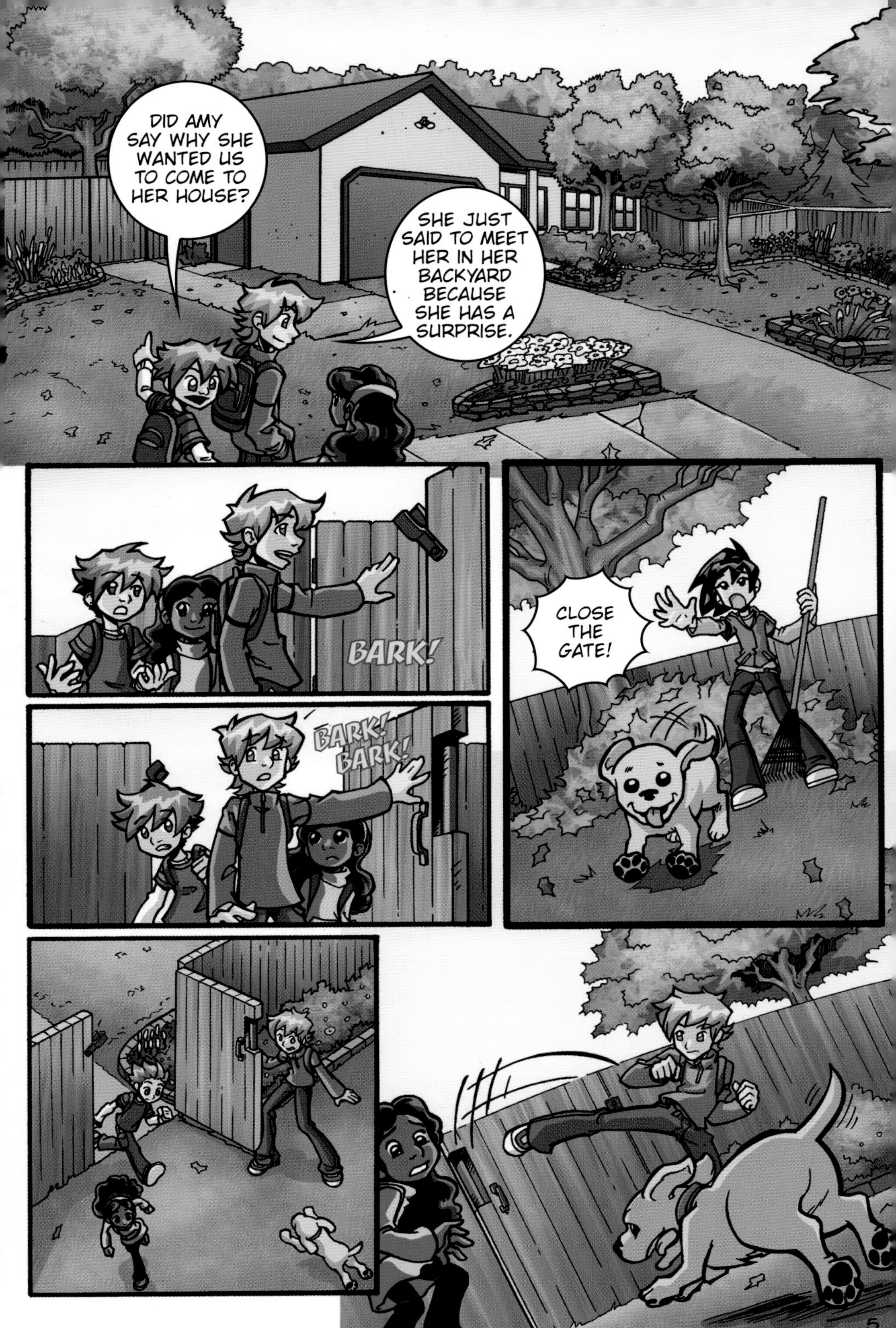
DID AMY SAY WHY SHE WANTED US TO COME TO HER HOUSE?
SHE JUST SAID TO MEET HER IN HER BACKYARD BECAUSE SHE HAS A SURPRISE.
BARK!
CLOSE THE GATE!
BARK! BARK!

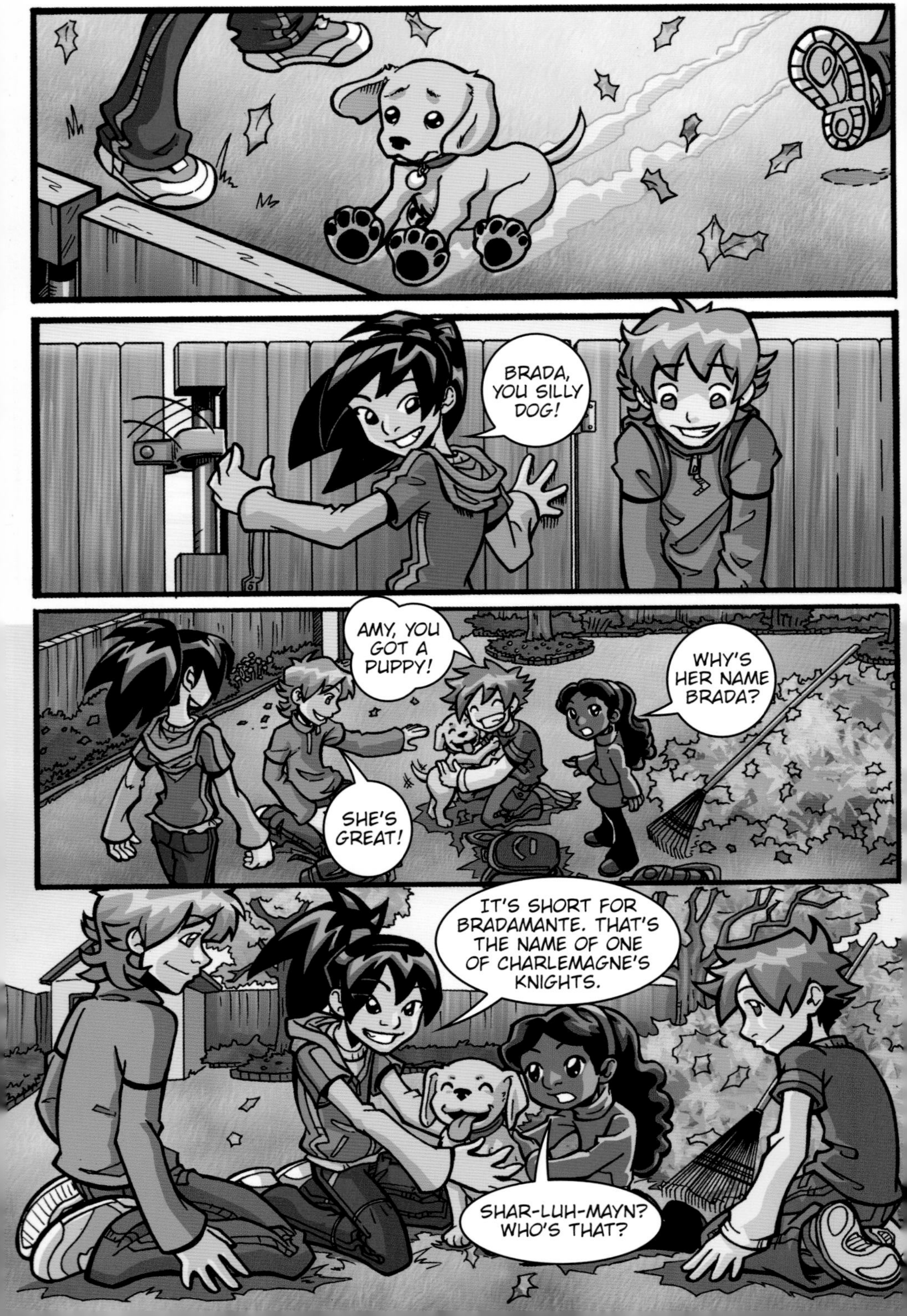
BRADA, YOU SILLY DOG!
AMY, YOU GOT A PUPPY!
SHE'S GREAT!
WHY'S HER NAME BRADA?
IT'S SHORT FOR BRADAMANTE. THAT'S THE NAME OF ONE OF CHARLEMAGNE'S KNIGHTS.
SHAR-LUH-MAYN? WHO'S THAT?

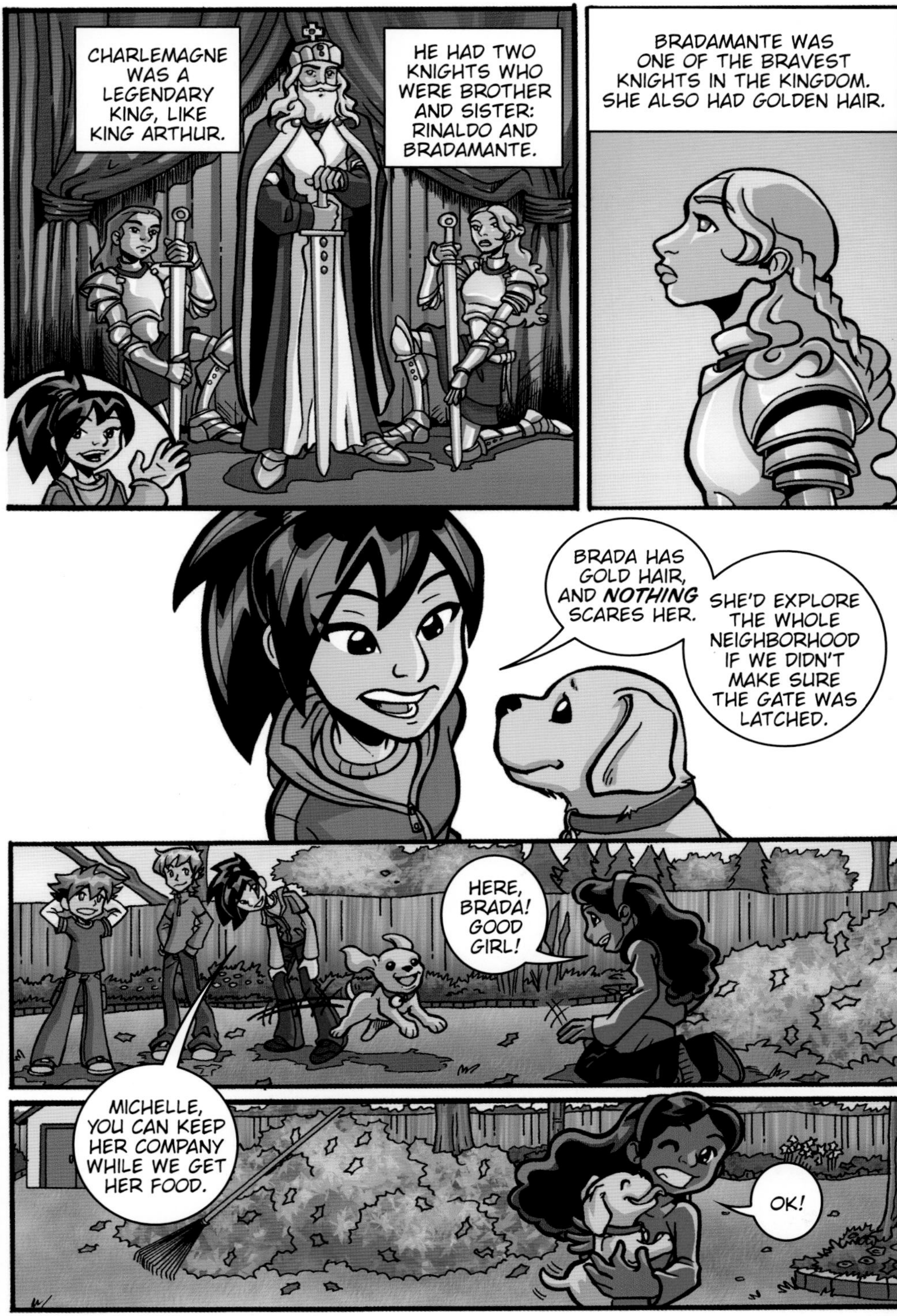
CHARLEMAGNE WAS A LEGENDARY KING, LIKE KING ARTHUR.
HE HAD TWO KNIGHTS WHO WERE BROTHER AND SISTER: RINALDO AND BRADAMANTE.
BRADAMANTE WAS ONE OF THE BRAVEST KNIGHTS IN THE KINGDOM. SHE ALSO HAD GOLDEN HAIR.
BRADA HAS GOLD HAIR, AND ***NOTHING*** SCARES HER.
SHE'D EXPLORE THE WHOLE NEIGHBORHOOD IF WE DIDN'T MAKE SURE THE GATE WAS LATCHED.
HERE, BRADA! GOOD GIRL!
MICHELLE, YOU CAN KEEP HER COMPANY WHILE WE GET HER FOOD.
OK!

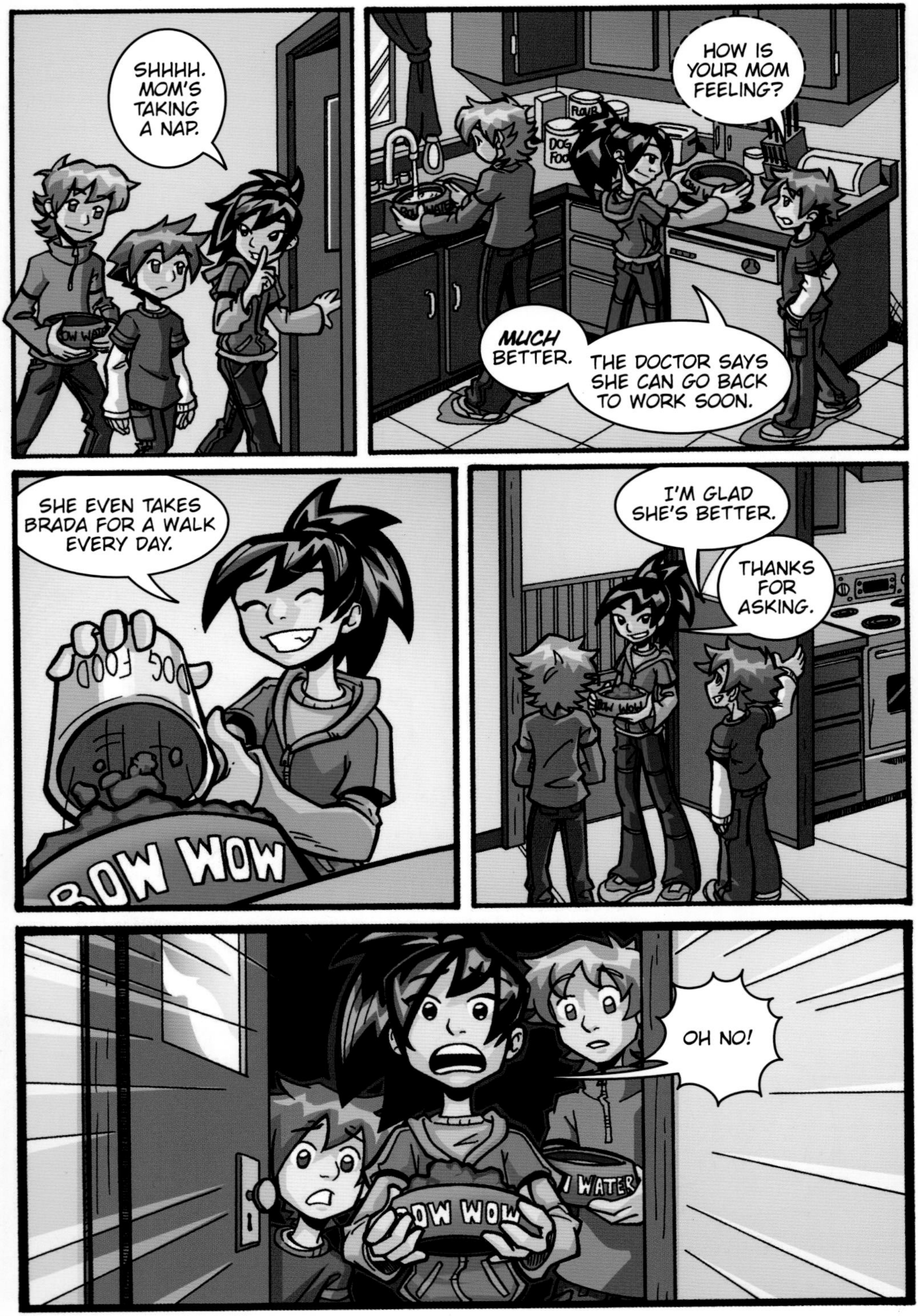
SHHHH. MOM'S TAKING A NAP.
HOW IS YOUR MOM FEELING?
FLOUR
DOG FOOD
BOW WATER
MUCH BETTER.
THE DOCTOR SAYS SHE CAN GO BACK TO WORK SOON.
SHE EVEN TAKES BRADA FOR A WALK EVERY DAY.
DOG FOOD
BOW WOW
I'M GLAD SHE'S BETTER.
THANKS FOR ASKING.
BOW WOW
OH NO!
BOW WOW
WATER

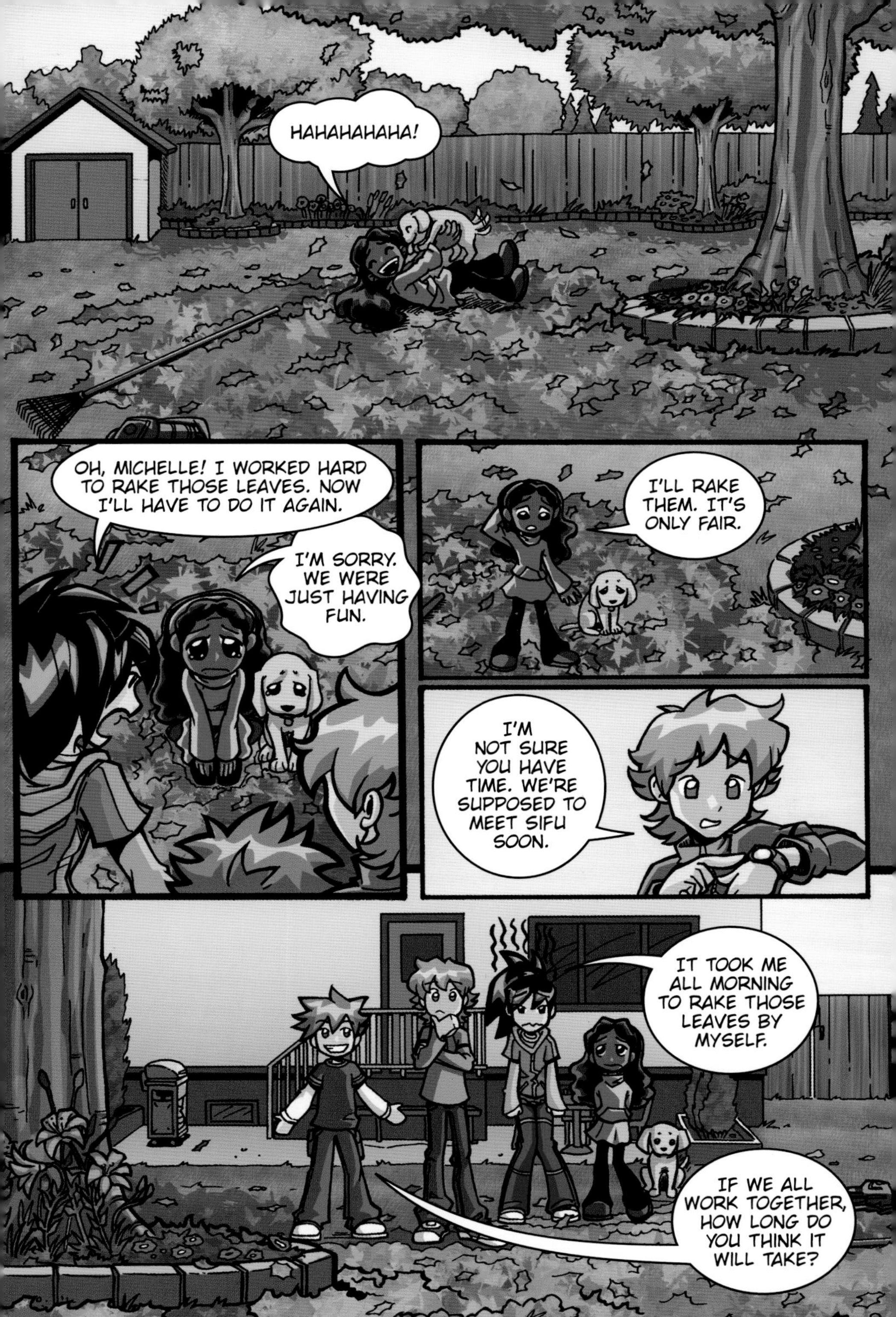
HAHAHAHAHA!
OH, MICHELLE! I WORKED HARD TO RAKE THOSE LEAVES. NOW I'LL HAVE TO DO IT AGAIN.
I'M SORRY. WE WERE JUST HAVING FUN.
I'LL RAKE THEM. IT'S ONLY FAIR.
I'M NOT SURE YOU HAVE TIME. WE'RE SUPPOSED TO MEET SIFU SOON.
IT TOOK ME ALL MORNING TO RAKE THOSE LEAVES BY MYSELF.
IF WE ALL WORK TOGETHER, HOW LONG DO YOU THINK IT WILL TAKE?

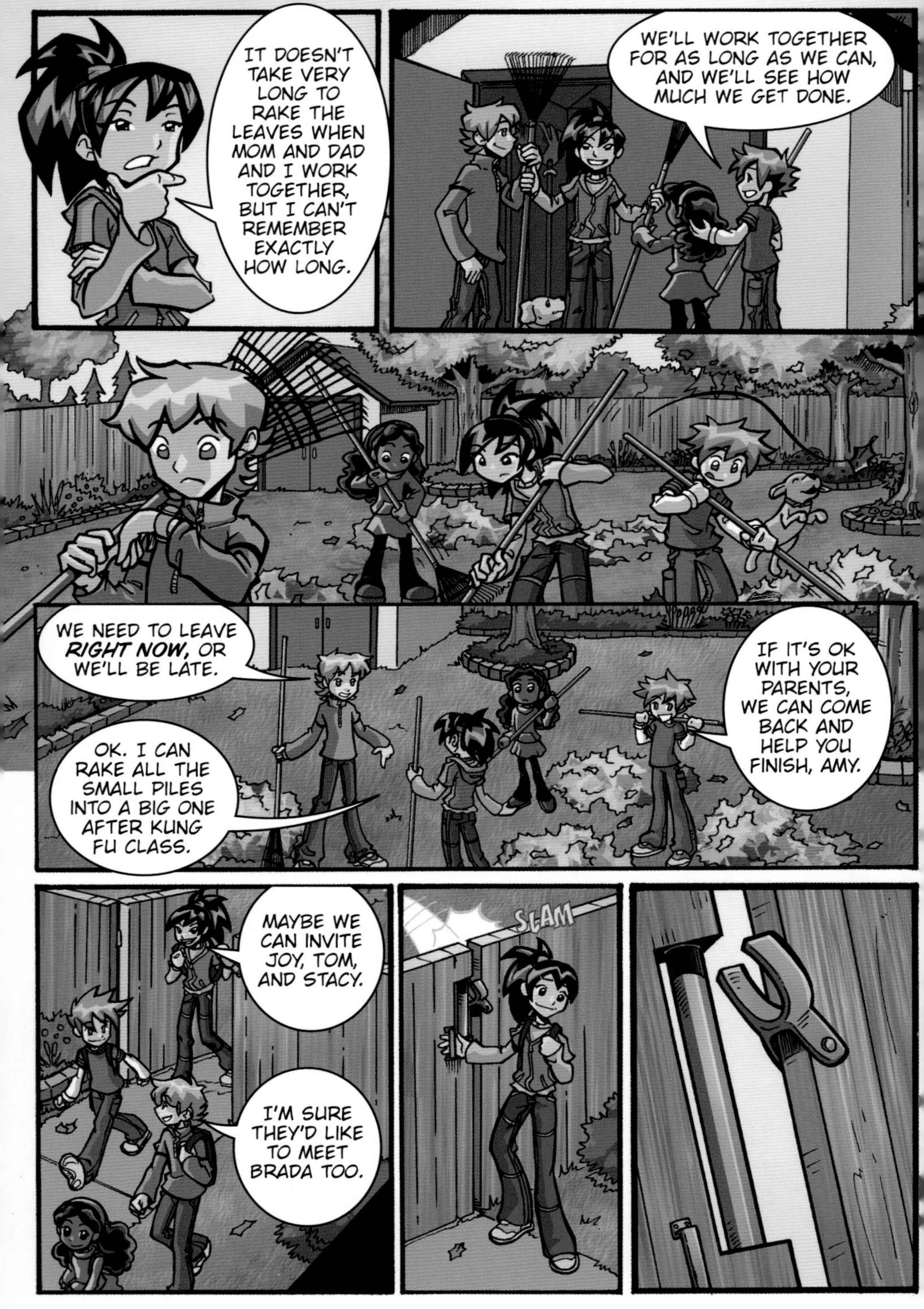
IT DOESN'T TAKE VERY LONG TO RAKE THE LEAVES WHEN MOM AND DAD AND I WORK TOGETHER, BUT I CAN'T REMEMBER EXACTLY HOW LONG.
WE'LL WORK TOGETHER FOR AS LONG AS WE CAN, AND WE'LL SEE HOW MUCH WE GET DONE.
WE NEED TO LEAVE ***RIGHT NOW,*** OR WE'LL BE LATE.
OK. I CAN RAKE ALL THE SMALL PILES INTO A BIG ONE AFTER KUNG FU CLASS.
IF IT'S OK WITH YOUR PARENTS, WE CAN COME BACK AND HELP YOU FINISH, AMY.
MAYBE WE CAN INVITE JOY, TOM, AND STACY.
I'M SURE THEY'D LIKE TO MEET BRADA TOO.
SLAM

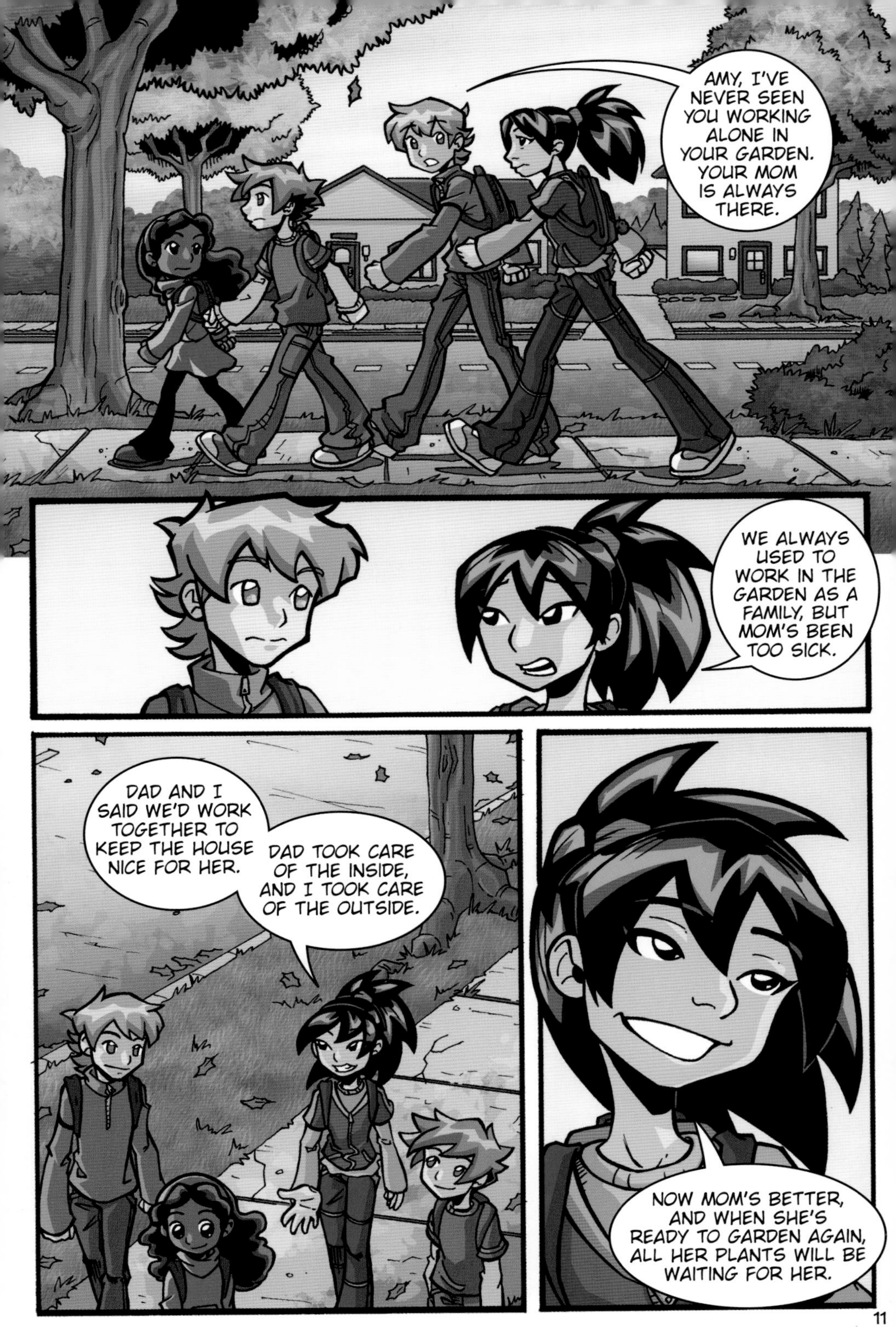
AMY, I'VE NEVER SEEN YOU WORKING ALONE IN YOUR GARDEN. YOUR MOM IS ALWAYS THERE.
WE ALWAYS USED TO WORK IN THE GARDEN AS A FAMILY, BUT MOM'S BEEN TOO SICK.
DAD AND I SAID WE'D WORK TOGETHER TO KEEP THE HOUSE NICE FOR HER.
DAD TOOK CARE OF THE INSIDE, AND I TOOK CARE OF THE OUTSIDE.
NOW MOM'S BETTER, AND WHEN SHE'S READY TO GARDEN AGAIN, ALL HER PLANTS WILL BE WAITING FOR HER.

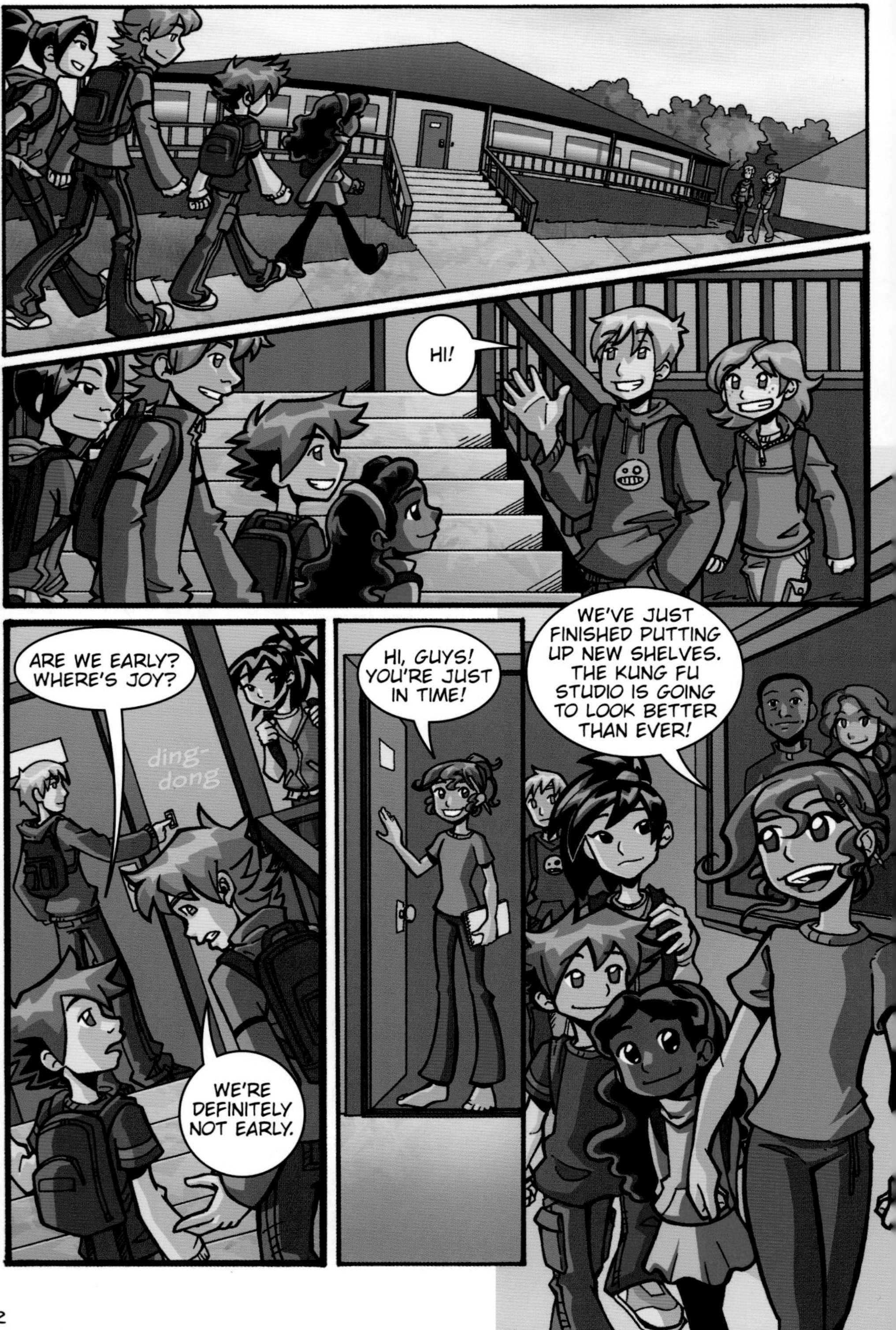
HI!
ARE WE EARLY? WHERE'S JOY?
ding-dong
WE'RE DEFINITELY NOT EARLY.
HI, GUYS! YOU'RE JUST IN TIME!
WE'VE JUST FINISHED PUTTING UP NEW SHELVES. THE KUNG FU STUDIO IS GOING TO LOOK BETTER THAN EVER!

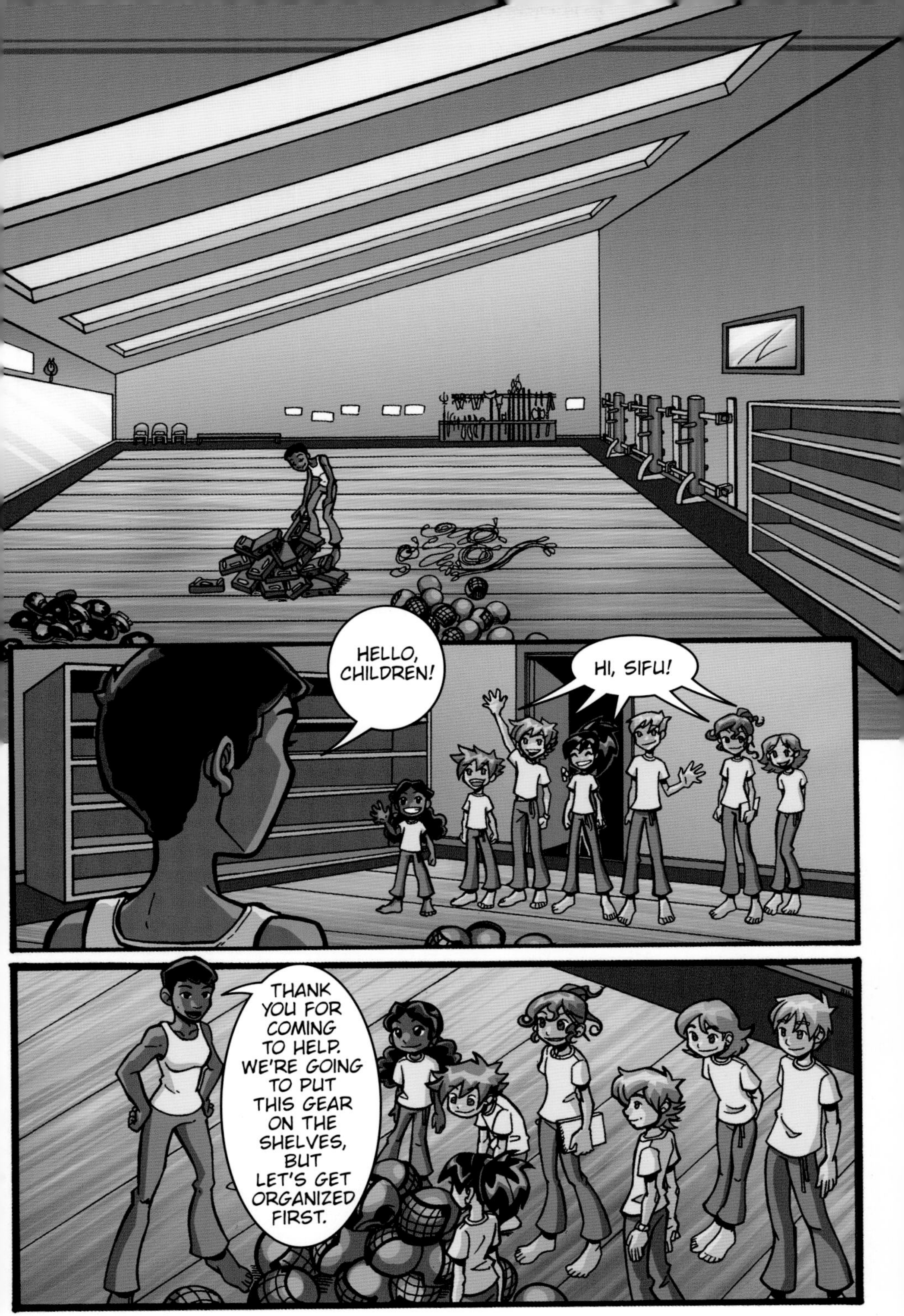
HELLO, CHILDREN!
HI, SIFU!
THANK YOU FOR COMING TO HELP. WE'RE GOING TO PUT THIS GEAR ON THE SHELVES, BUT LET'S GET ORGANIZED FIRST.

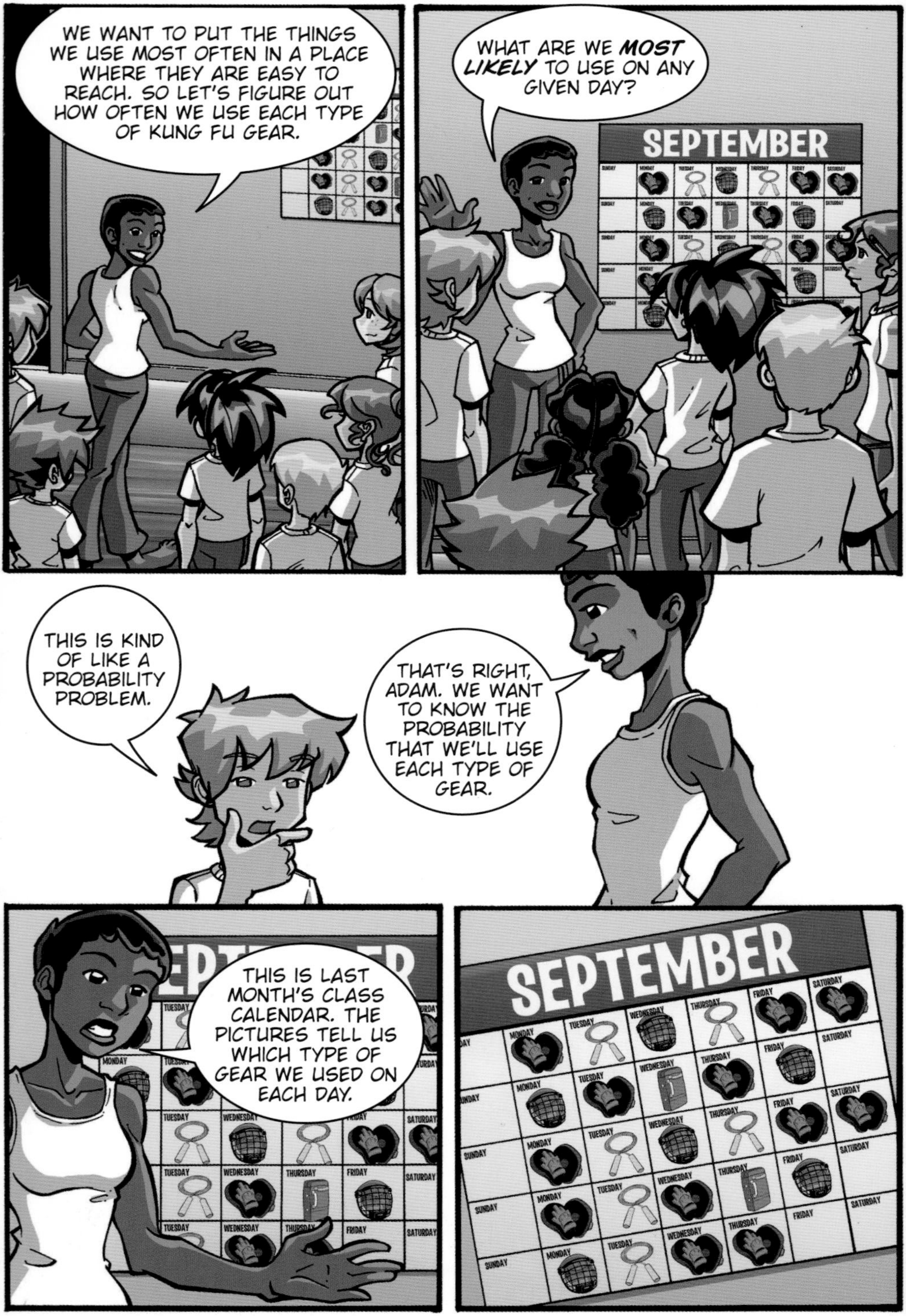
WE WANT TO PUT THE THINGS WE USE MOST OFTEN IN A PLACE WHERE THEY ARE EASY TO REACH. SO LET'S FIGURE OUT HOW OFTEN WE USE EACH TYPE OF KUNG FU GEAR.
WHAT ARE WE ***MOST LIKELY*** TO USE ON ANY GIVEN DAY?
SEPTEMBER
THIS IS KIND OF LIKE A PROBABILITY PROBLEM.
THAT'S RIGHT, ADAM. WE WANT TO KNOW THE PROBABILITY THAT WE'LL USE EACH TYPE OF GEAR.
THIS IS LAST MONTH'S CLASS CALENDAR. THE PICTURES TELL US WHICH TYPE OF GEAR WE USED ON EACH DAY.
SEPTEMBER

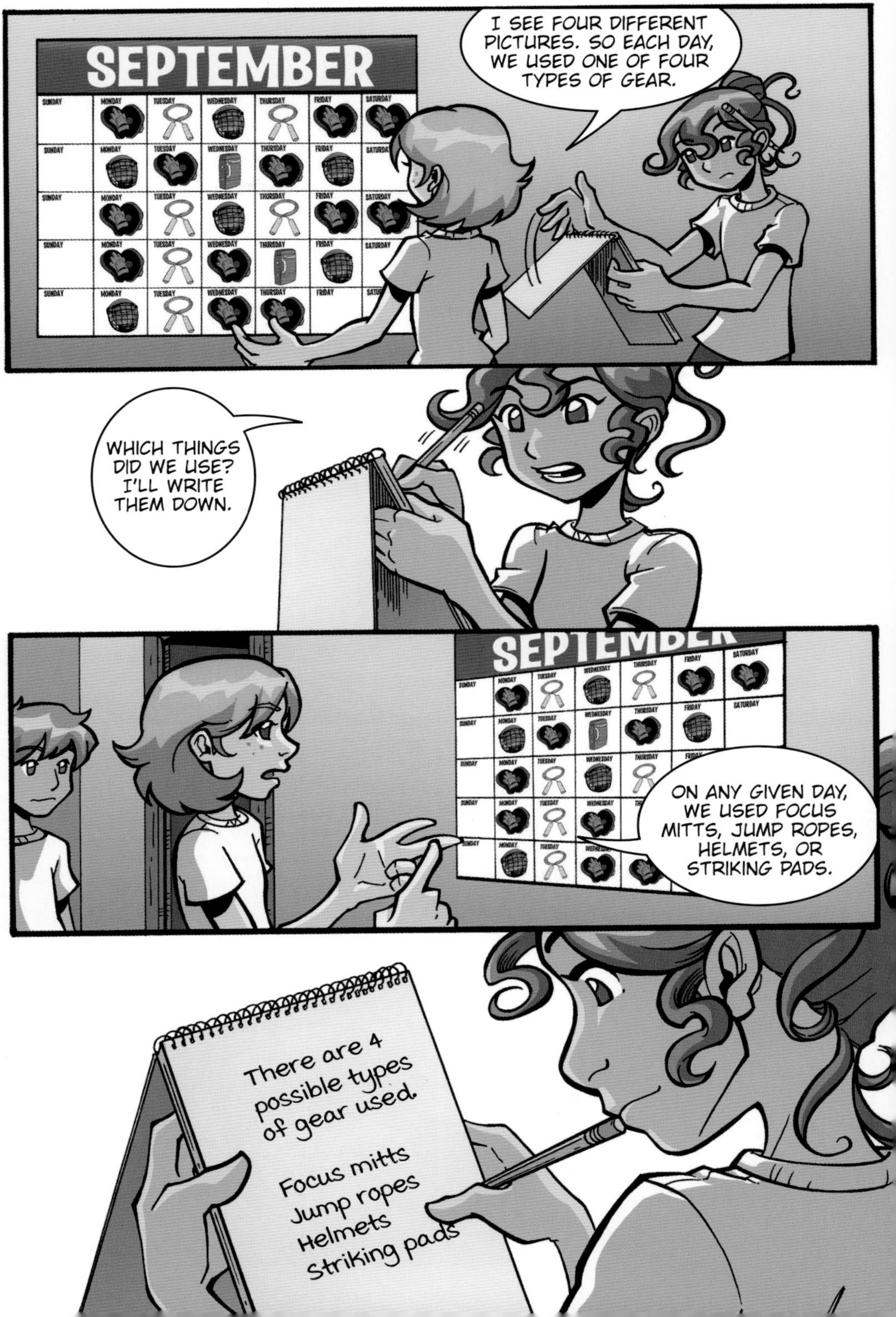
SEPTEMBER
I SEE FOUR DIFFERENT PICTURES. SO EACH DAY, WE USED ONE OF FOUR TYPES OF GEAR.
WHICH THINGS DID WE USE? I'LL WRITE THEM DOWN.
SEPTEMBER
ON ANY GIVEN DAY, WE USED FOCUS MITTS, JUMP ROPES, HELMETS, OR STRIKING PADS.
There are 4 possible types of gear used.
Focus mitts
Jump ropes
Helmets
Striking pads

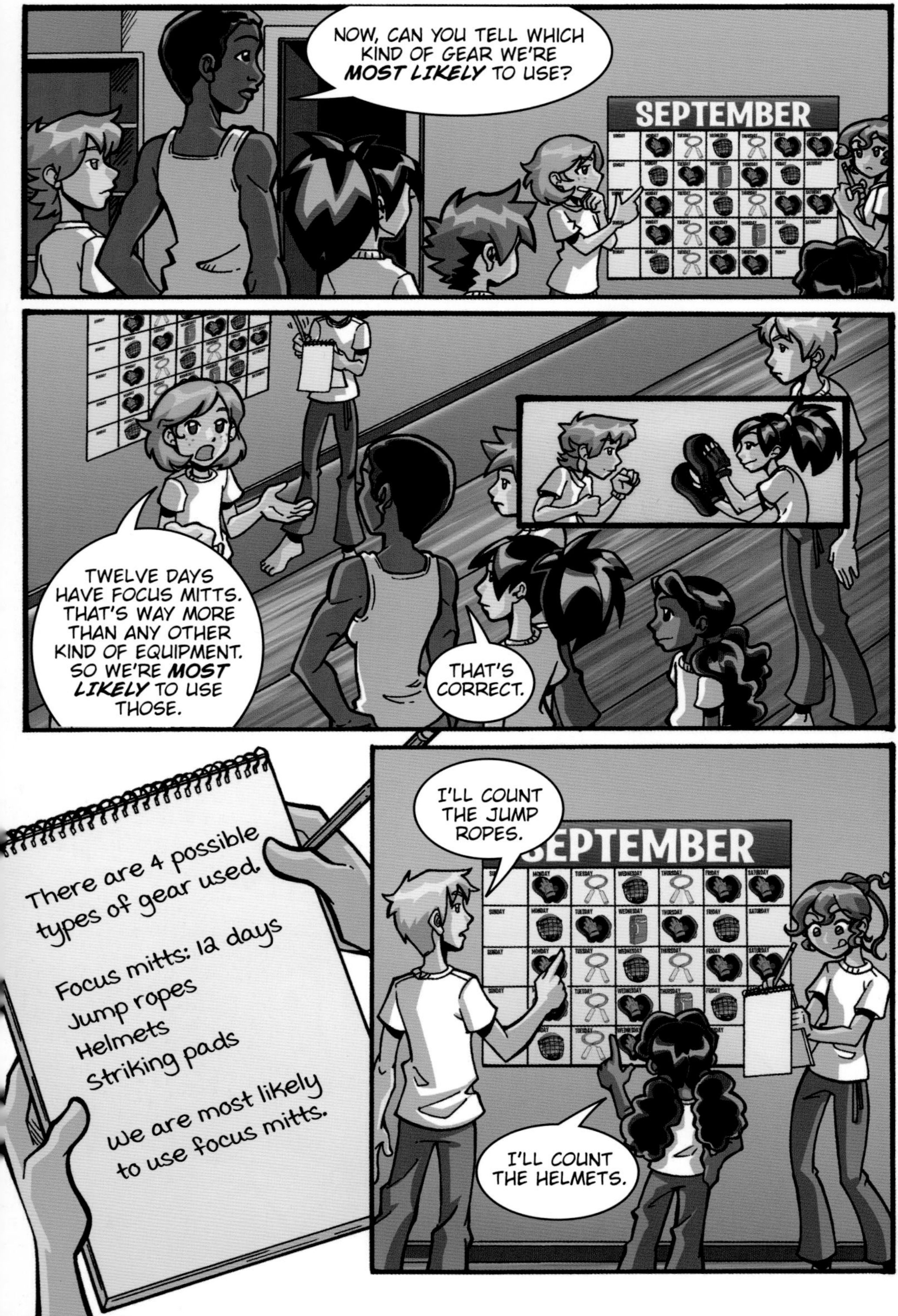
NOW, CAN YOU TELL WHICH KIND OF GEAR WE'RE **MOST LIKELY** TO USE?
SEPTEMBER
TWELVE DAYS HAVE FOCUS MITTS. THAT'S WAY MORE THAN ANY OTHER KIND OF EQUIPMENT. SO WE'RE **MOST LIKELY** TO USE THOSE.
THAT'S CORRECT.
There are 4 possible types of gear used.
Focus mitts: 12 days
Jump ropes
Helmets
Striking pads
We are most likely to use focus mitts.
I'LL COUNT THE JUMP ROPES.
SEPTEMBER
I'LL COUNT THE HELMETS.

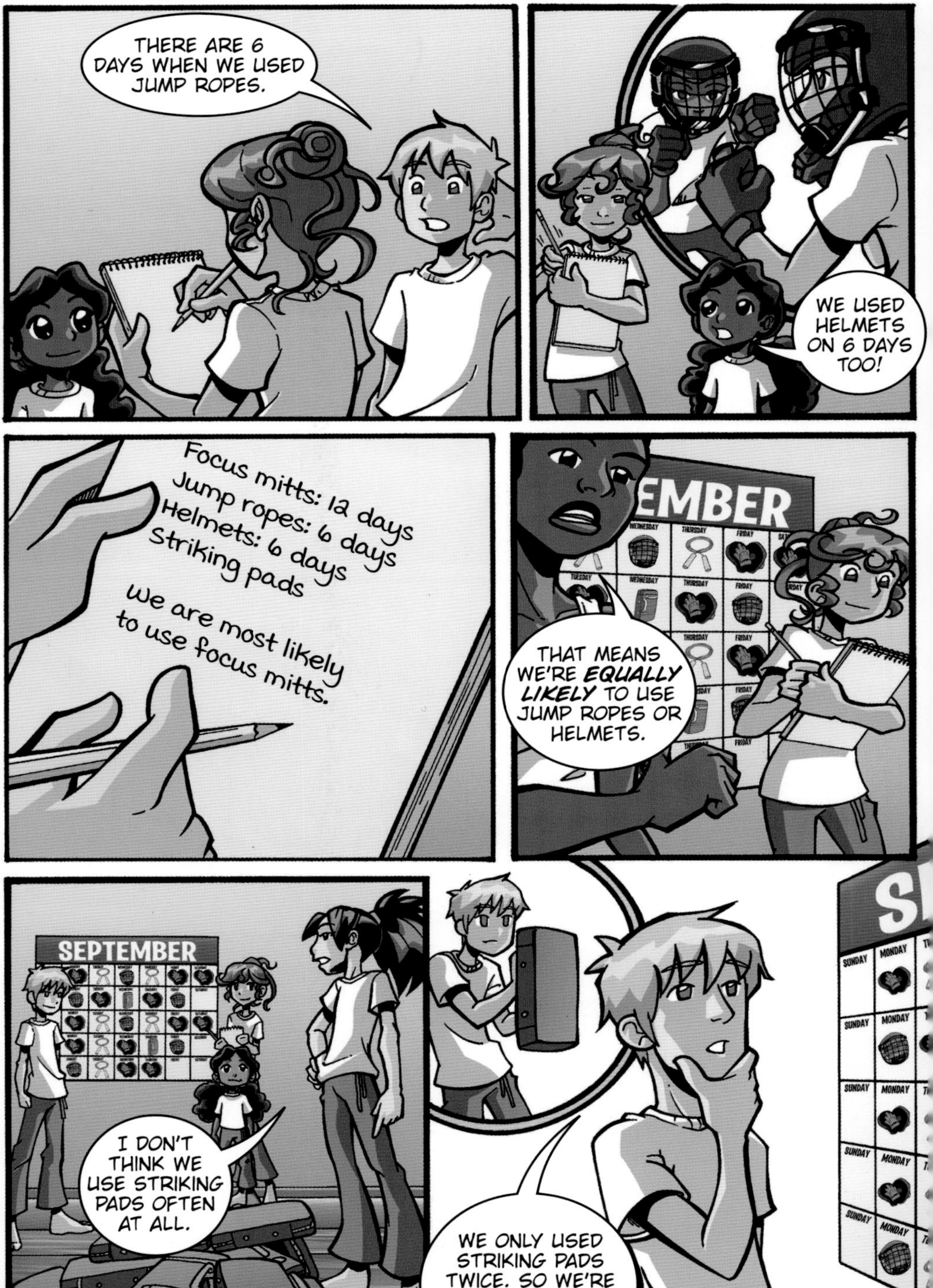

THERE ARE 6 DAYS WHEN WE USED JUMP ROPES.
WE USED HELMETS ON 6 DAYS TOO!
Focus mitts: 12 days
Jump ropes: 6 days
Helmets: 6 days
Striking pads
We are most likely to use focus mitts.
EMBER
THAT MEANS WE'RE ***EQUALLY LIKELY*** TO USE JUMP ROPES OR HELMETS.
SEPTEMBER
I DON'T THINK WE USE STRIKING PADS OFTEN AT ALL.
WE ONLY USED STRIKING PADS TWICE. SO WE'RE ***LEAST LIKELY*** TO USE STRIKING PADS.

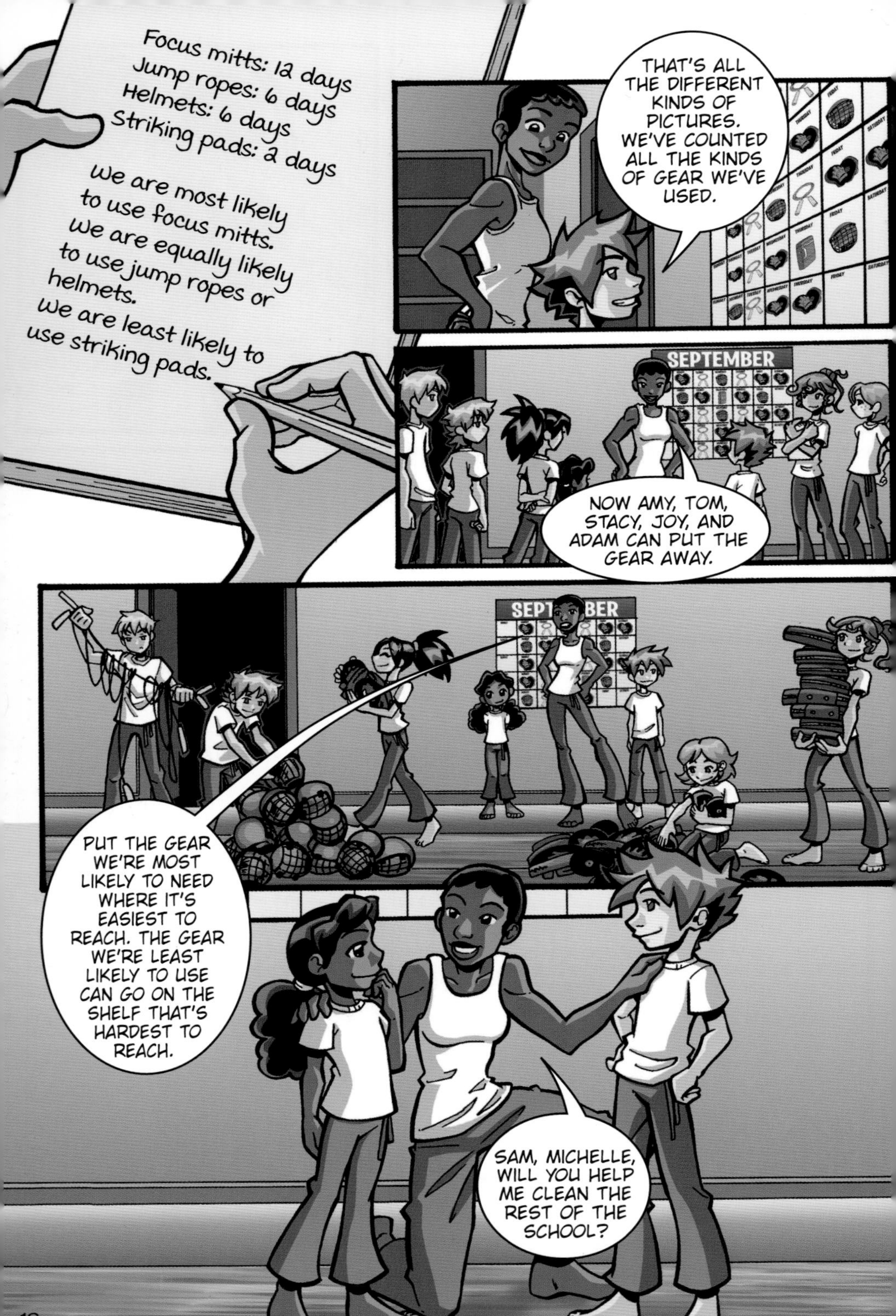
Focus mitts: 12 days
Jump ropes: 6 days
Helmets: 6 days
Striking pads: 2 days
We are most likely to use focus mitts.
We are equally likely to use jump ropes or helmets.
We are least likely to use striking pads.
THAT'S ALL THE DIFFERENT KINDS OF PICTURES. WE'VE COUNTED ALL THE KINDS OF GEAR WE'VE USED.
SEPTEMBER
NOW AMY, TOM, STACY, JOY, AND ADAM CAN PUT THE GEAR AWAY.
SEPTEMBER
PUT THE GEAR WE'RE MOST LIKELY TO NEED WHERE IT'S EASIEST TO REACH. THE GEAR WE'RE LEAST LIKELY TO USE CAN GO ON THE SHELF THAT'S HARDEST TO REACH.
SAM, MICHELLE, WILL YOU HELP ME CLEAN THE REST OF THE SCHOOL?

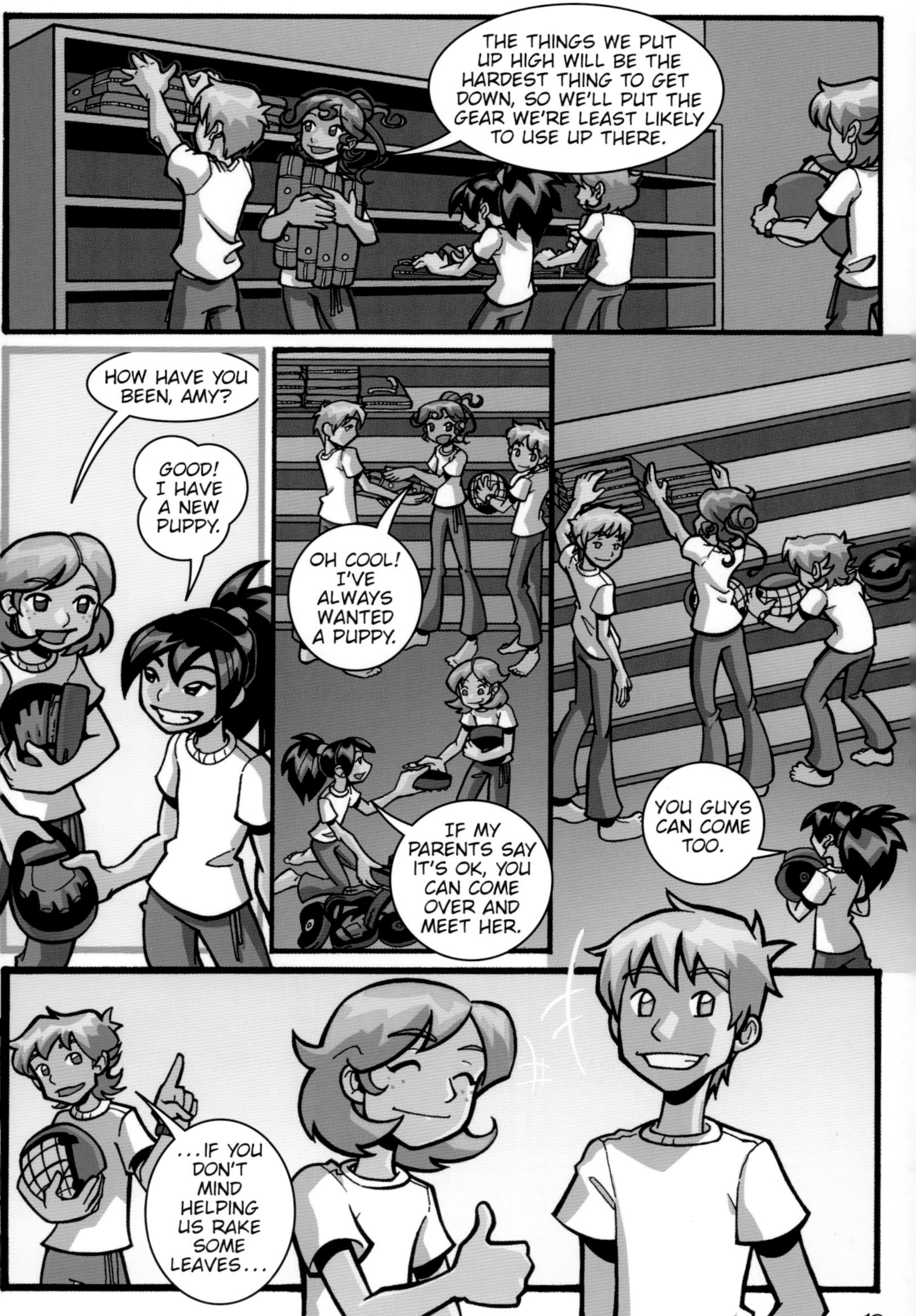
THE THINGS WE PUT UP HIGH WILL BE THE HARDEST THING TO GET DOWN, SO WE'LL PUT THE GEAR WE'RE LEAST LIKELY TO USE UP THERE.
HOW HAVE YOU BEEN, AMY?
GOOD! I HAVE A NEW PUPPY.
OH COOL! I'VE ALWAYS WANTED A PUPPY.
IF MY PARENTS SAY IT'S OK, YOU CAN COME OVER AND MEET HER.
YOU GUYS CAN COME TOO.
...IF YOU DON'T MIND HELPING US RAKE SOME LEAVES...

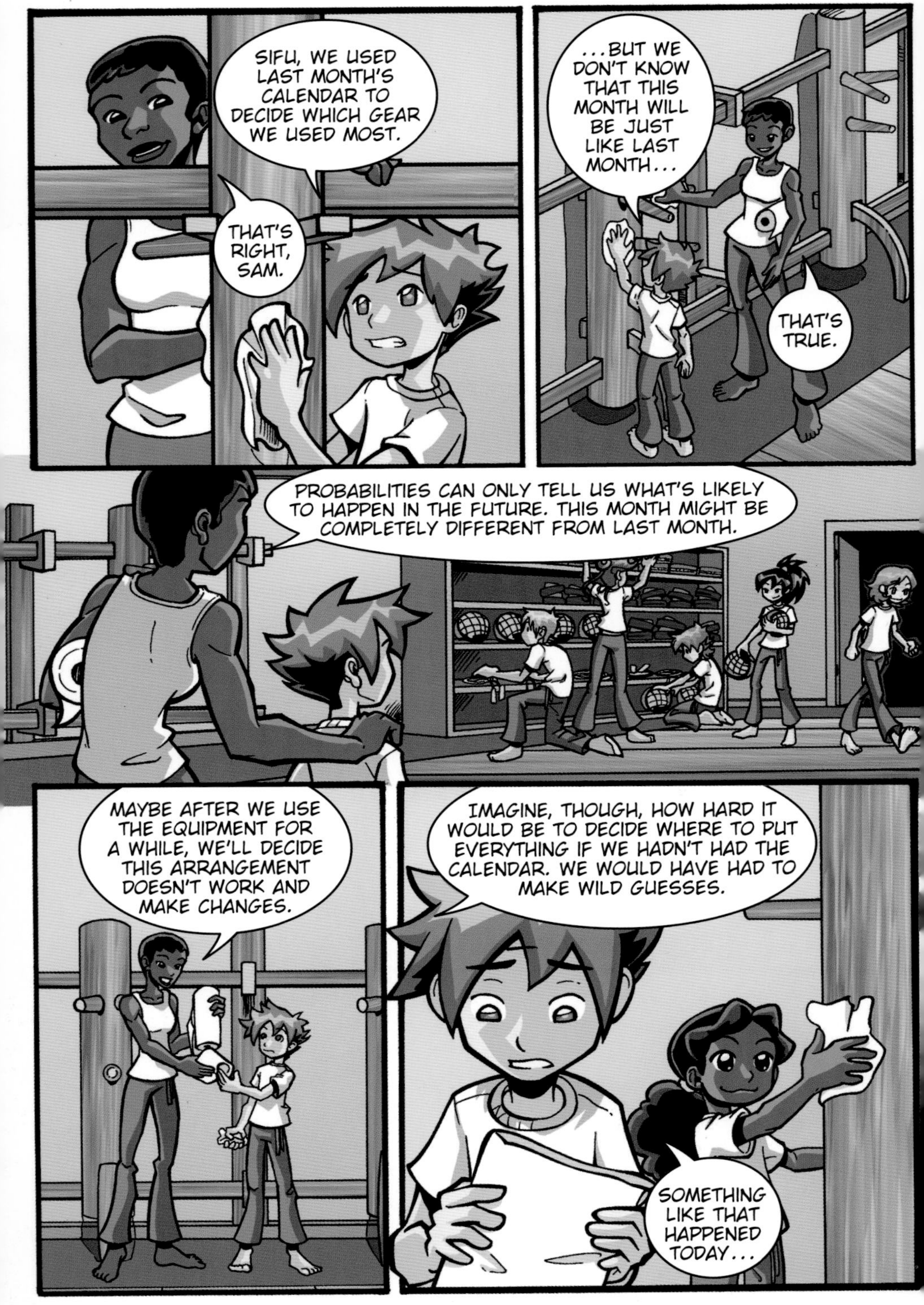
SIFU, WE USED LAST MONTH'S CALENDAR TO DECIDE WHICH GEAR WE USED MOST.
THAT'S RIGHT, SAM.
. . . BUT WE DON'T KNOW THAT THIS MONTH WILL BE JUST LIKE LAST MONTH . . .
THAT'S TRUE.
PROBABILITIES CAN ONLY TELL US WHAT'S LIKELY TO HAPPEN IN THE FUTURE. THIS MONTH MIGHT BE COMPLETELY DIFFERENT FROM LAST MONTH.
MAYBE AFTER WE USE THE EQUIPMENT FOR A WHILE, WE'LL DECIDE THIS ARRANGEMENT DOESN'T WORK AND MAKE CHANGES.
IMAGINE, THOUGH, HOW HARD IT WOULD BE TO DECIDE WHERE TO PUT EVERYTHING IF WE HADN'T HAD THE CALENDAR. WE WOULD HAVE HAD TO MAKE WILD GUESSES.
SOMETHING LIKE THAT HAPPENED TODAY . . .

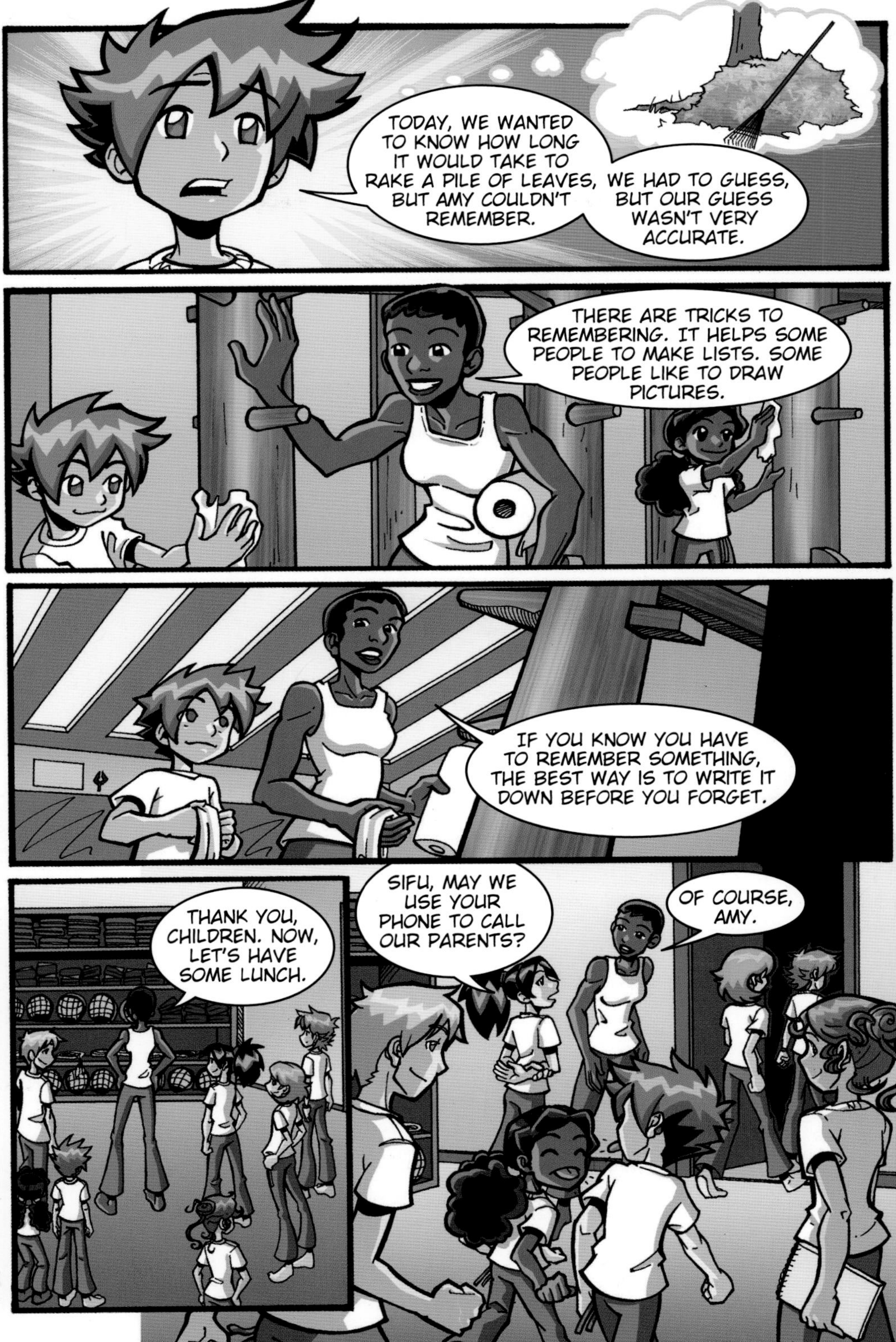
TODAY, WE WANTED TO KNOW HOW LONG IT WOULD TAKE TO RAKE A PILE OF LEAVES, BUT AMY COULDN'T REMEMBER.
WE HAD TO GUESS, BUT OUR GUESS WASN'T VERY ACCURATE.
THERE ARE TRICKS TO REMEMBERING. IT HELPS SOME PEOPLE TO MAKE LISTS. SOME PEOPLE LIKE TO DRAW PICTURES.
IF YOU KNOW YOU HAVE TO REMEMBER SOMETHING, THE BEST WAY IS TO WRITE IT DOWN BEFORE YOU FORGET.
THANK YOU, CHILDREN. NOW, LET'S HAVE SOME LUNCH.
SIFU, MAY WE USE YOUR PHONE TO CALL OUR PARENTS?
OF COURSE, AMY.

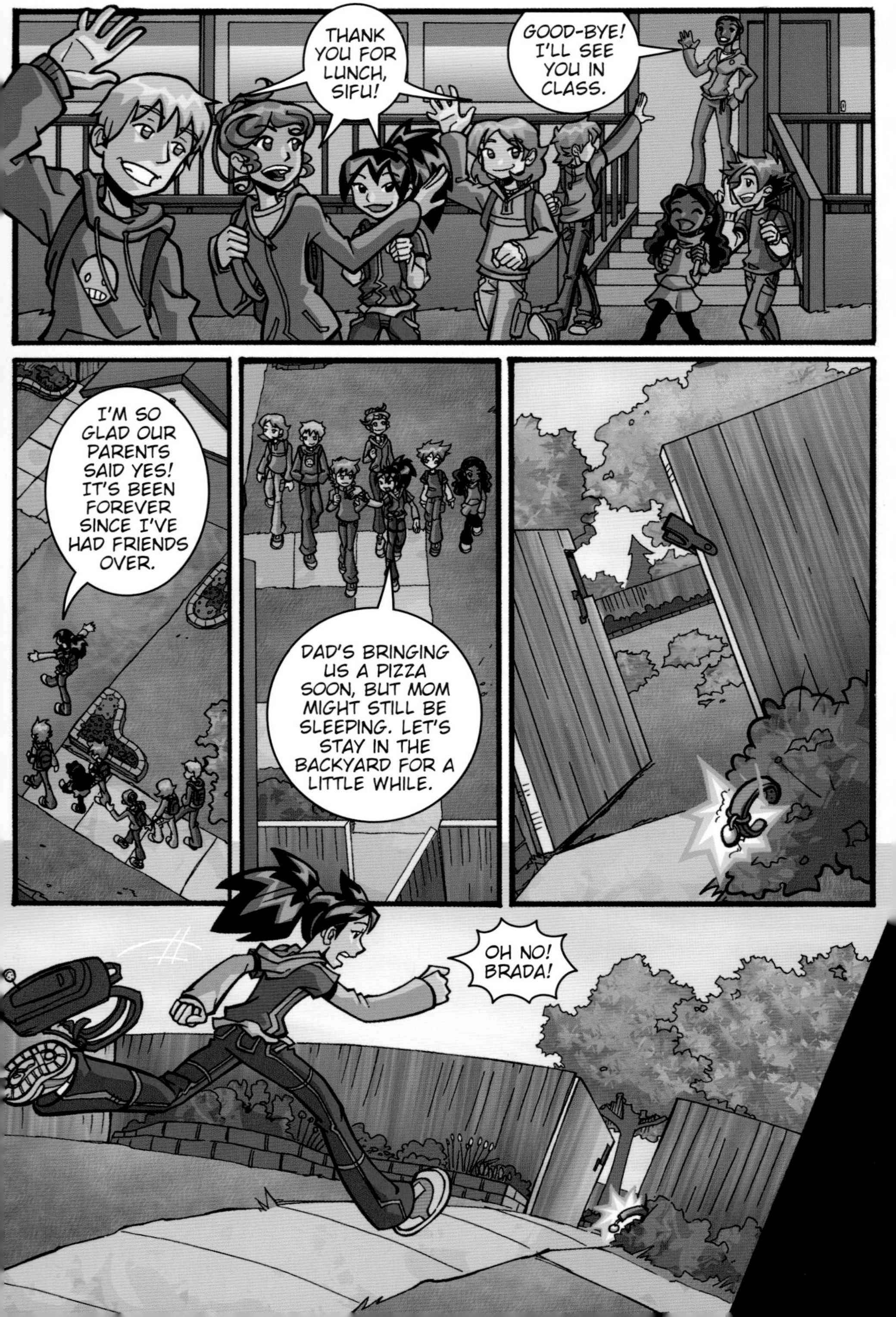
THANK YOU FOR LUNCH, SIFU!
GOOD-BYE! I'LL SEE YOU IN CLASS.
I'M SO GLAD OUR PARENTS SAID YES! IT'S BEEN FOREVER SINCE I'VE HAD FRIENDS OVER.
DAD'S BRINGING US A PIZZA SOON, BUT MOM MIGHT STILL BE SLEEPING. LET'S STAY IN THE BACKYARD FOR A LITTLE WHILE.
OH NO! BRADA!

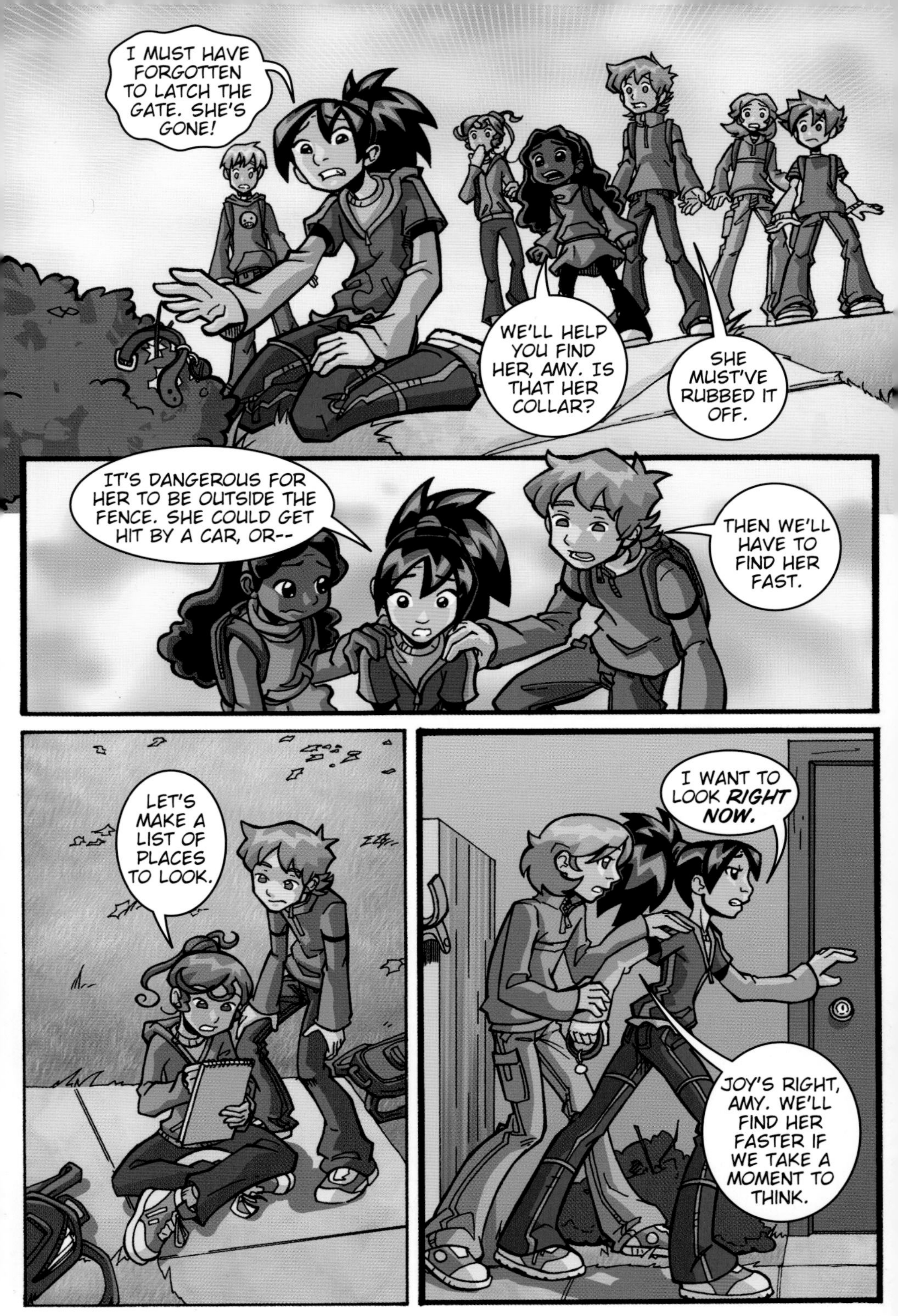
I MUST HAVE FORGOTTEN TO LATCH THE GATE. SHE'S GONE!
WE'LL HELP YOU FIND HER, AMY. IS THAT HER COLLAR?
SHE MUST'VE RUBBED IT OFF.
IT'S DANGEROUS FOR HER TO BE OUTSIDE THE FENCE. SHE COULD GET HIT BY A CAR, OR--
THEN WE'LL HAVE TO FIND HER FAST.
LET'S MAKE A LIST OF PLACES TO LOOK.
I WANT TO LOOK ***RIGHT NOW.***
JOY'S RIGHT, AMY. WE'LL FIND HER FASTER IF WE TAKE A MOMENT TO THINK.

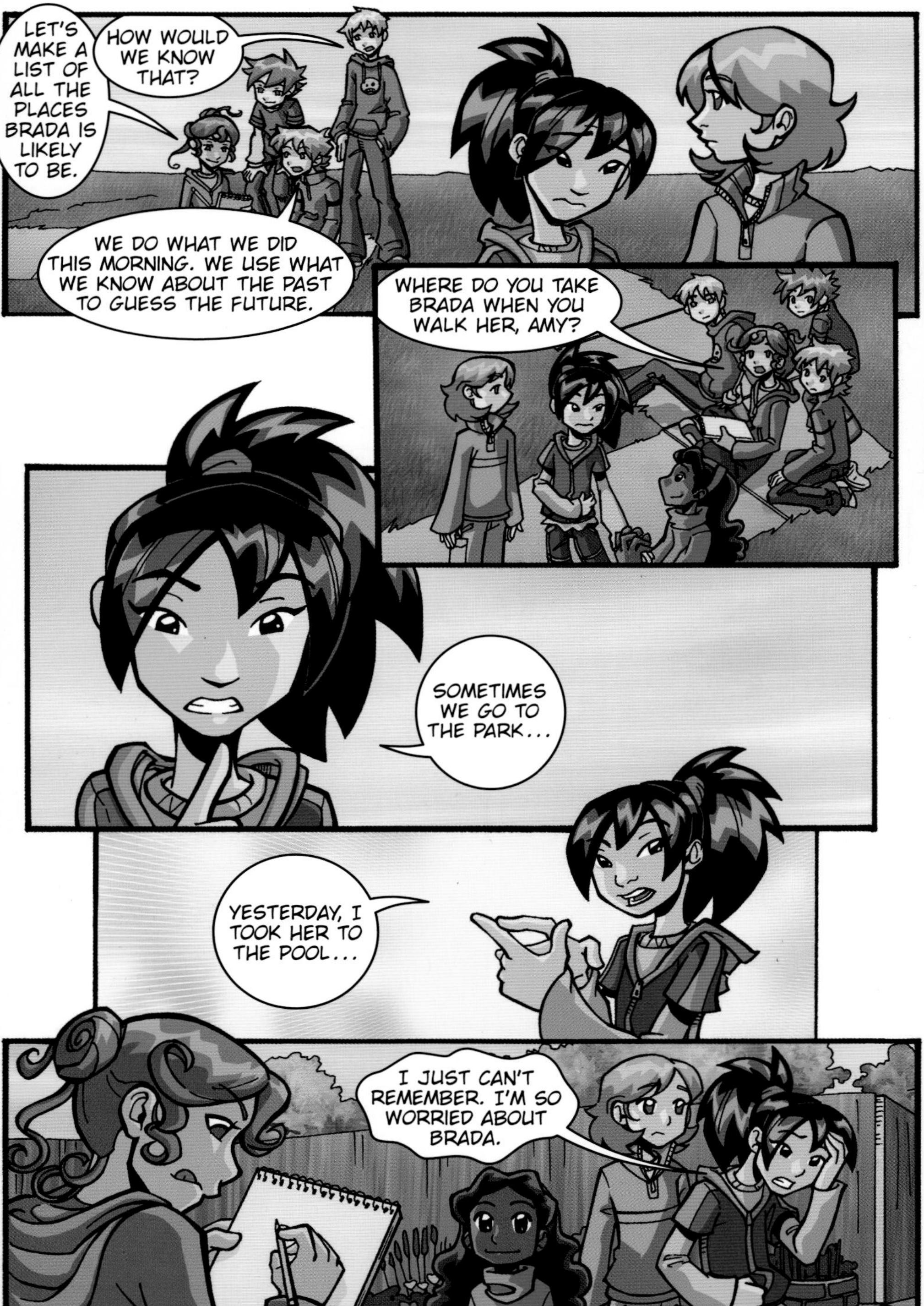
LET'S MAKE A LIST OF ALL THE PLACES BRADA IS LIKELY TO BE.
HOW WOULD WE KNOW THAT?
WE DO WHAT WE DID THIS MORNING. WE USE WHAT WE KNOW ABOUT THE PAST TO GUESS THE FUTURE.
WHERE DO YOU TAKE BRADA WHEN YOU WALK HER, AMY?
SOMETIMES WE GO TO THE PARK...
YESTERDAY, I TOOK HER TO THE POOL...
I JUST CAN'T REMEMBER. I'M SO WORRIED ABOUT BRADA.

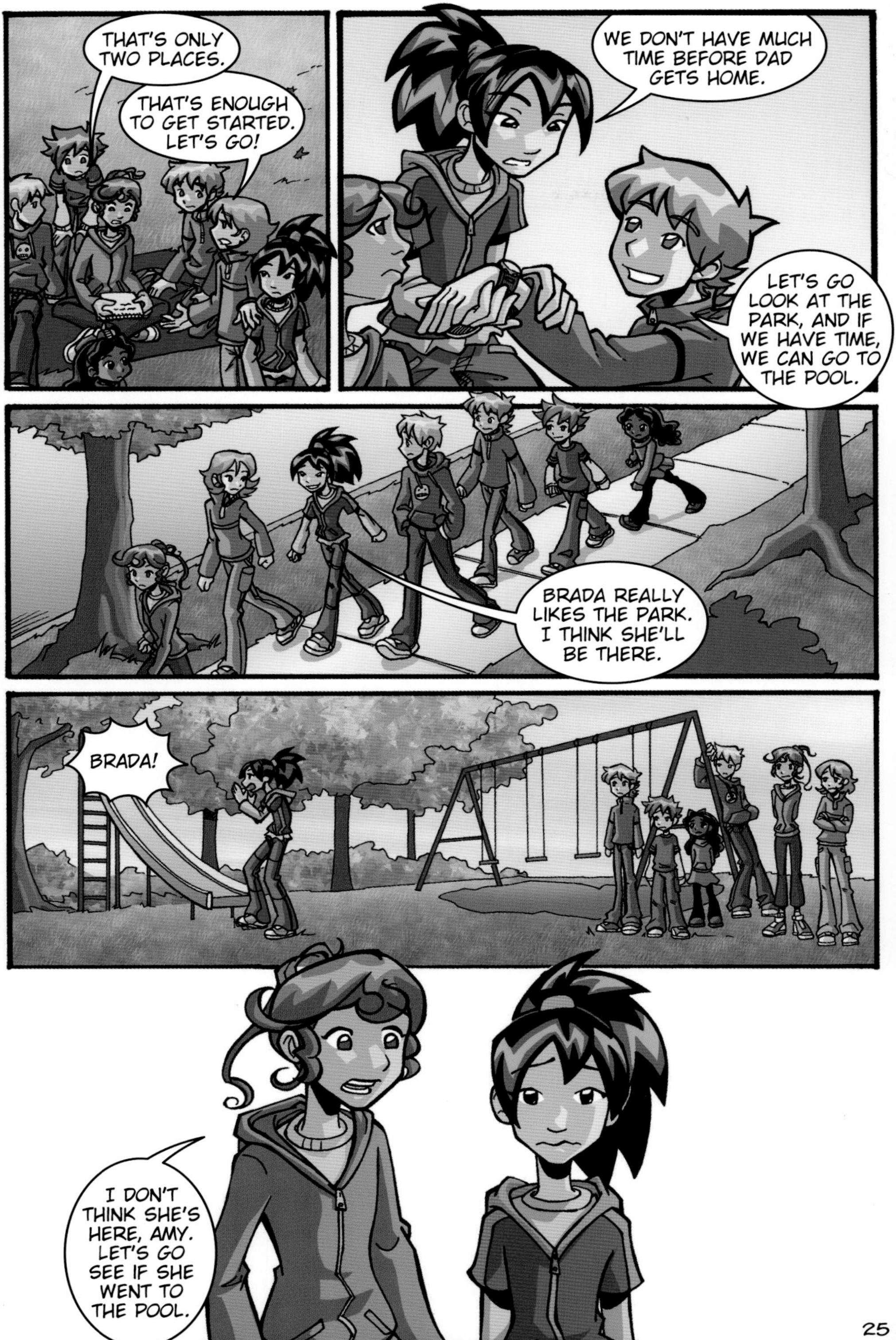
THAT'S ONLY TWO PLACES.
THAT'S ENOUGH TO GET STARTED. LET'S GO!
WE DON'T HAVE MUCH TIME BEFORE DAD GETS HOME.
LET'S GO LOOK AT THE PARK, AND IF WE HAVE TIME, WE CAN GO TO THE POOL.
BRADA REALLY LIKES THE PARK. I THINK SHE'LL BE THERE.
BRADA!
I DON'T THINK SHE'S HERE, AMY. LET'S GO SEE IF SHE WENT TO THE POOL.

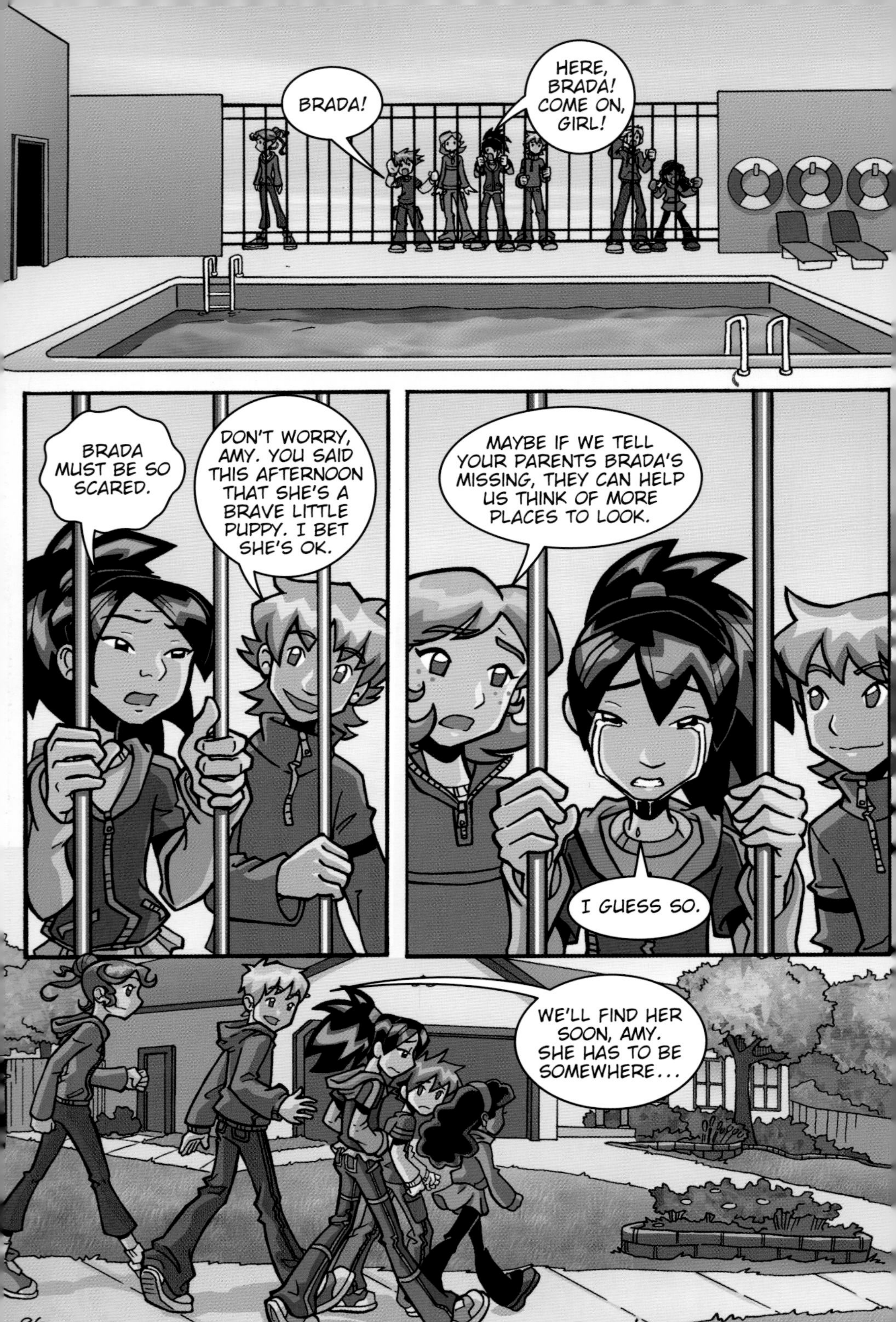
BRADA!
HERE, BRADA! COME ON, GIRL!
BRADA MUST BE SO SCARED.
DON'T WORRY, AMY. YOU SAID THIS AFTERNOON THAT SHE'S A BRAVE LITTLE PUPPY. I BET SHE'S OK.
MAYBE IF WE TELL YOUR PARENTS BRADA'S MISSING, THEY CAN HELP US THINK OF MORE PLACES TO LOOK.
I GUESS SO.
WE'LL FIND HER SOON, AMY. SHE HAS TO BE SOMEWHERE...

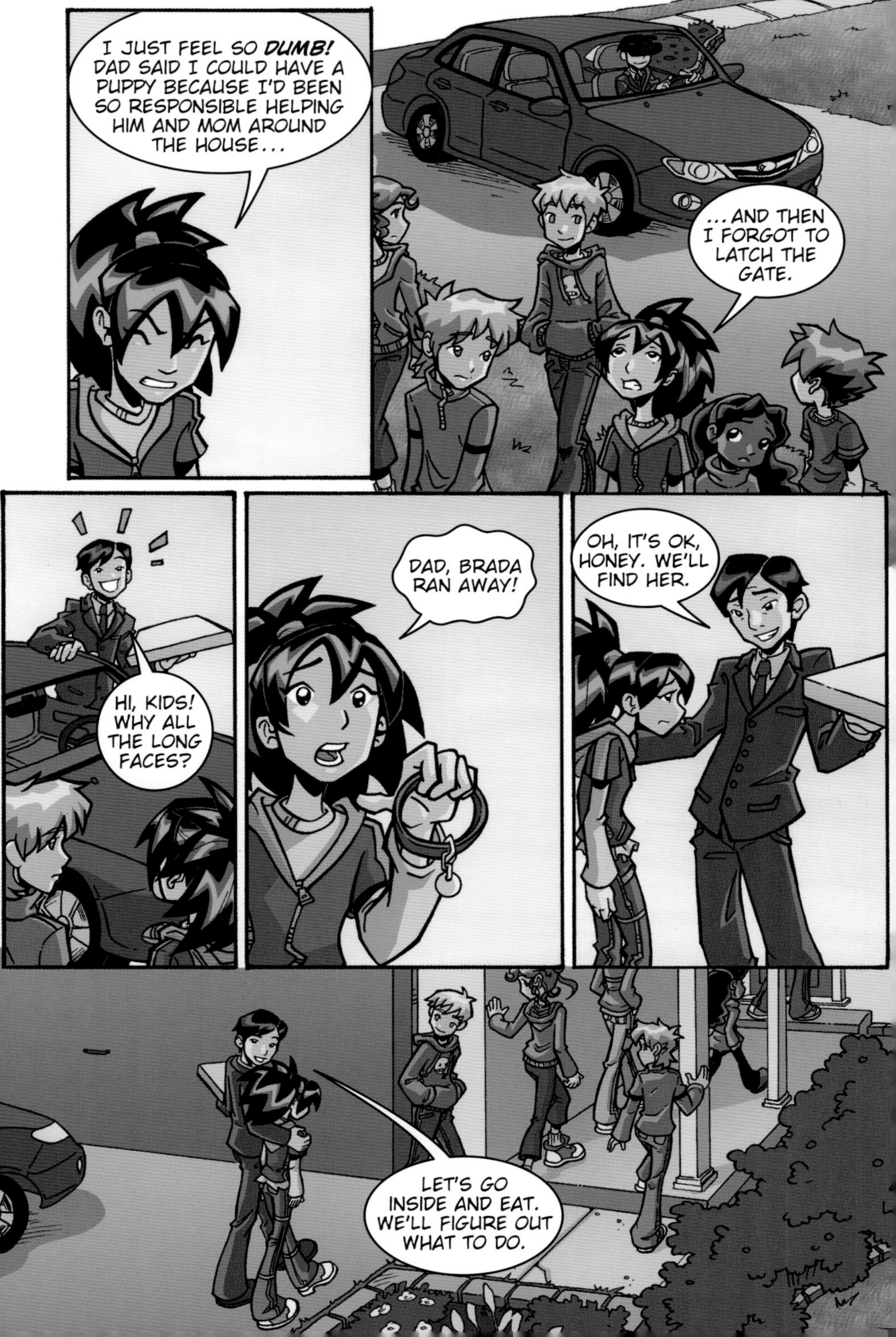
I JUST FEEL SO DUMB! DAD SAID I COULD HAVE A PUPPY BECAUSE I'D BEEN SO RESPONSIBLE HELPING HIM AND MOM AROUND THE HOUSE...
...AND THEN I FORGOT TO LATCH THE GATE.
HI, KIDS! WHY ALL THE LONG FACES?
DAD, BRADA RAN AWAY!
OH, IT'S OK, HONEY. WE'LL FIND HER.
LET'S GO INSIDE AND EAT. WE'LL FIGURE OUT WHAT TO DO.

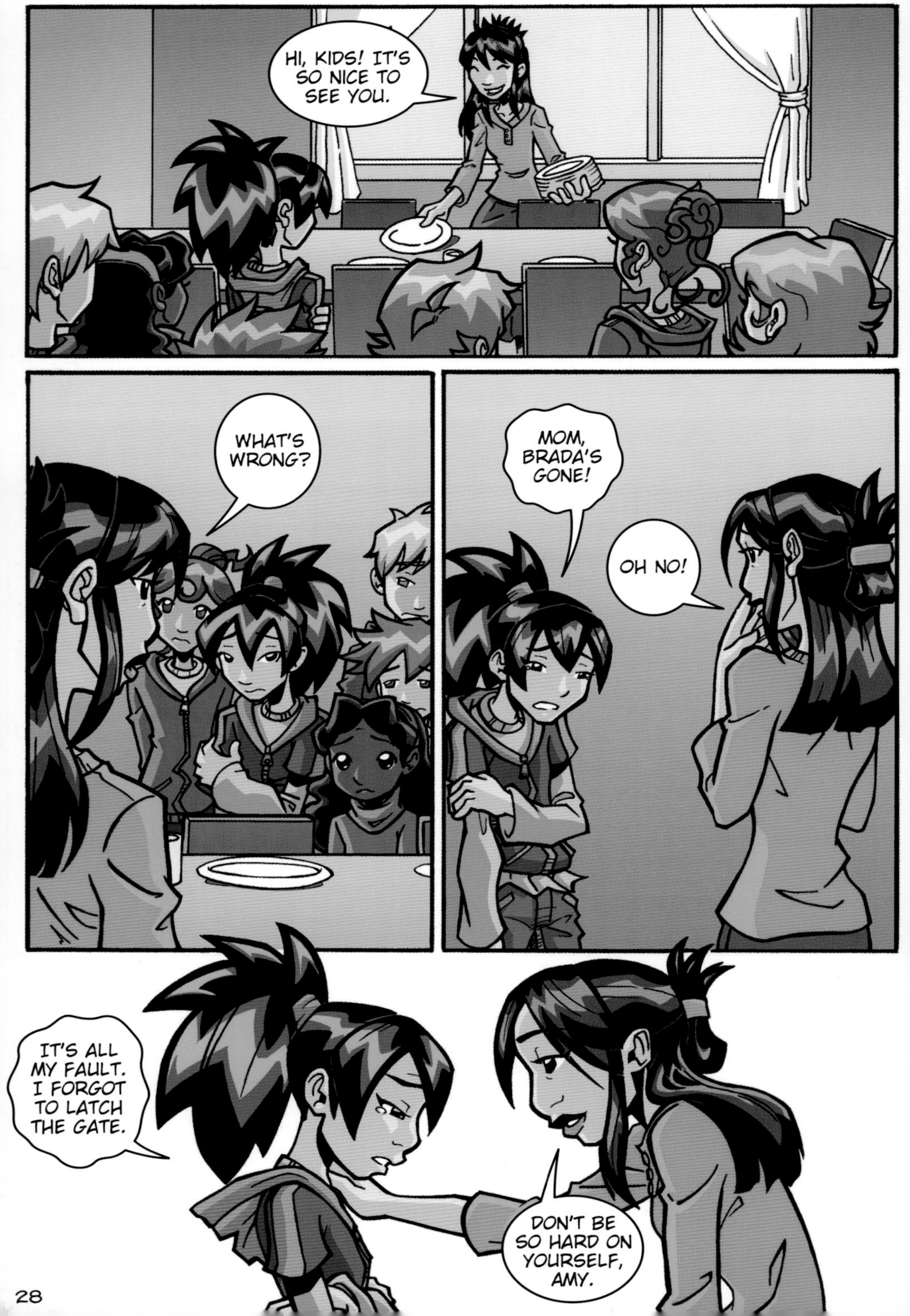
HI, KIDS! IT'S SO NICE TO SEE YOU.
WHAT'S WRONG?
MOM, BRADA'S GONE!
OH NO!
IT'S ALL MY FAULT. I FORGOT TO LATCH THE GATE.
DON'T BE SO HARD ON YOURSELF, AMY.

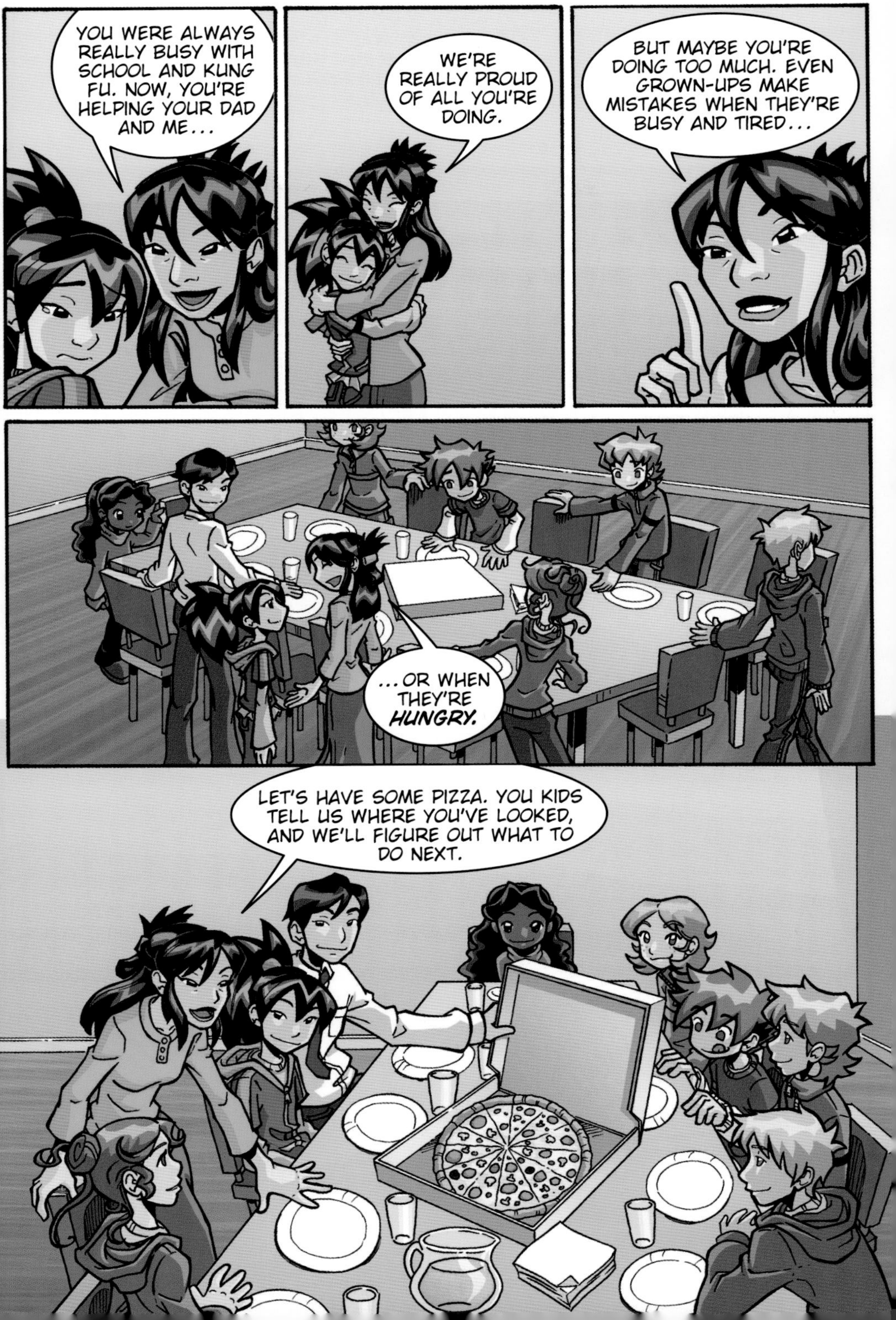
YOU WERE ALWAYS REALLY BUSY WITH SCHOOL AND KUNG FU. NOW, YOU'RE HELPING YOUR DAD AND ME...
WE'RE REALLY PROUD OF ALL YOU'RE DOING.
BUT MAYBE YOU'RE DOING TOO MUCH. EVEN GROWN-UPS MAKE MISTAKES WHEN THEY'RE BUSY AND TIRED...
...OR WHEN THEY'RE ***HUNGRY.***
LET'S HAVE SOME PIZZA. YOU KIDS TELL US WHERE YOU'VE LOOKED, AND WE'LL FIGURE OUT WHAT TO DO NEXT.

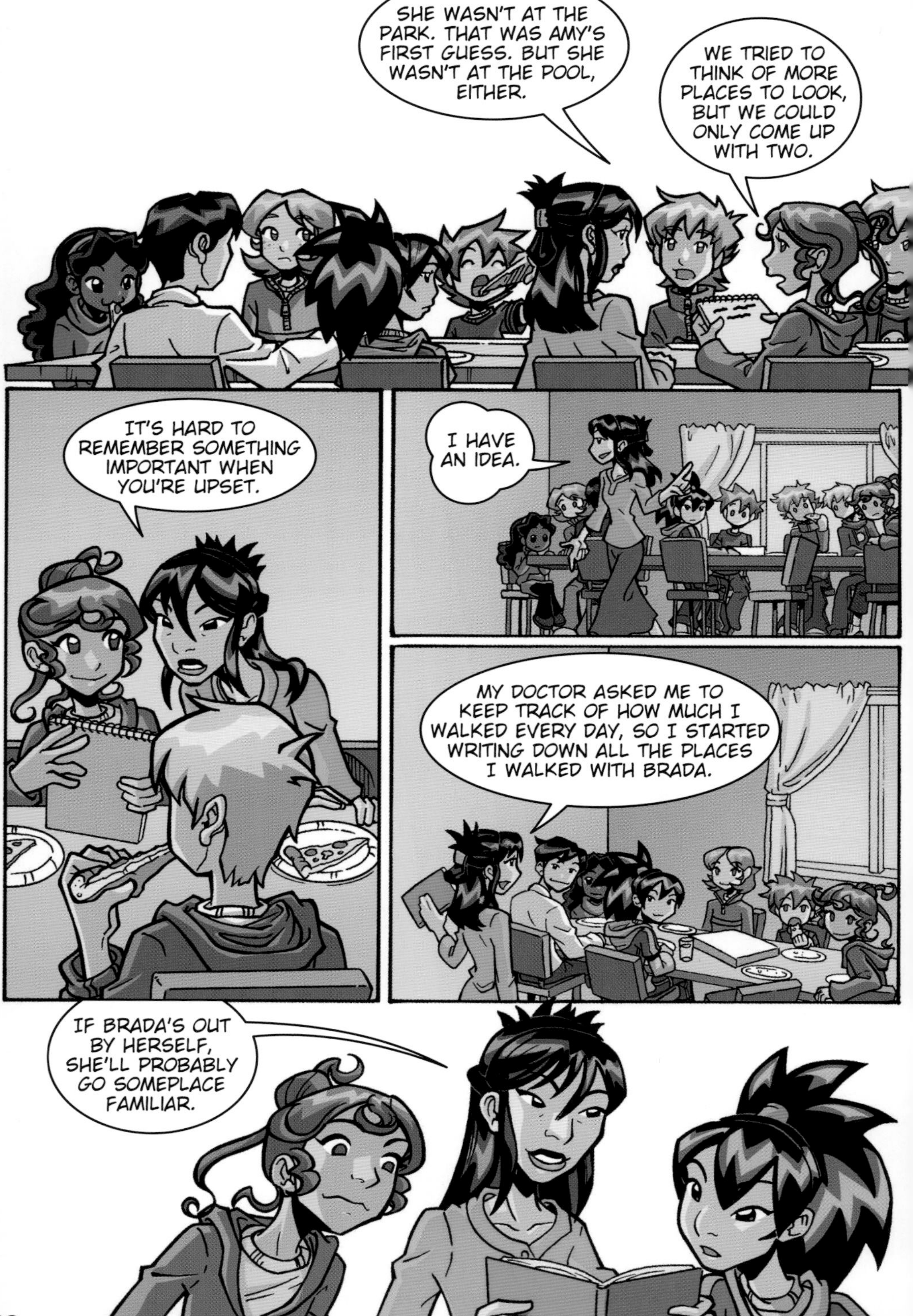
SHE WASN'T AT THE PARK. THAT WAS AMY'S FIRST GUESS. BUT SHE WASN'T AT THE POOL, EITHER.
WE TRIED TO THINK OF MORE PLACES TO LOOK, BUT WE COULD ONLY COME UP WITH TWO.
IT'S HARD TO REMEMBER SOMETHING IMPORTANT WHEN YOU'RE UPSET.
I HAVE AN IDEA.
MY DOCTOR ASKED ME TO KEEP TRACK OF HOW MUCH I WALKED EVERY DAY, SO I STARTED WRITING DOWN ALL THE PLACES I WALKED WITH BRADA.
IF BRADA'S OUT BY HERSELF, SHE'LL PROBABLY GO SOMEPLACE FAMILIAR.

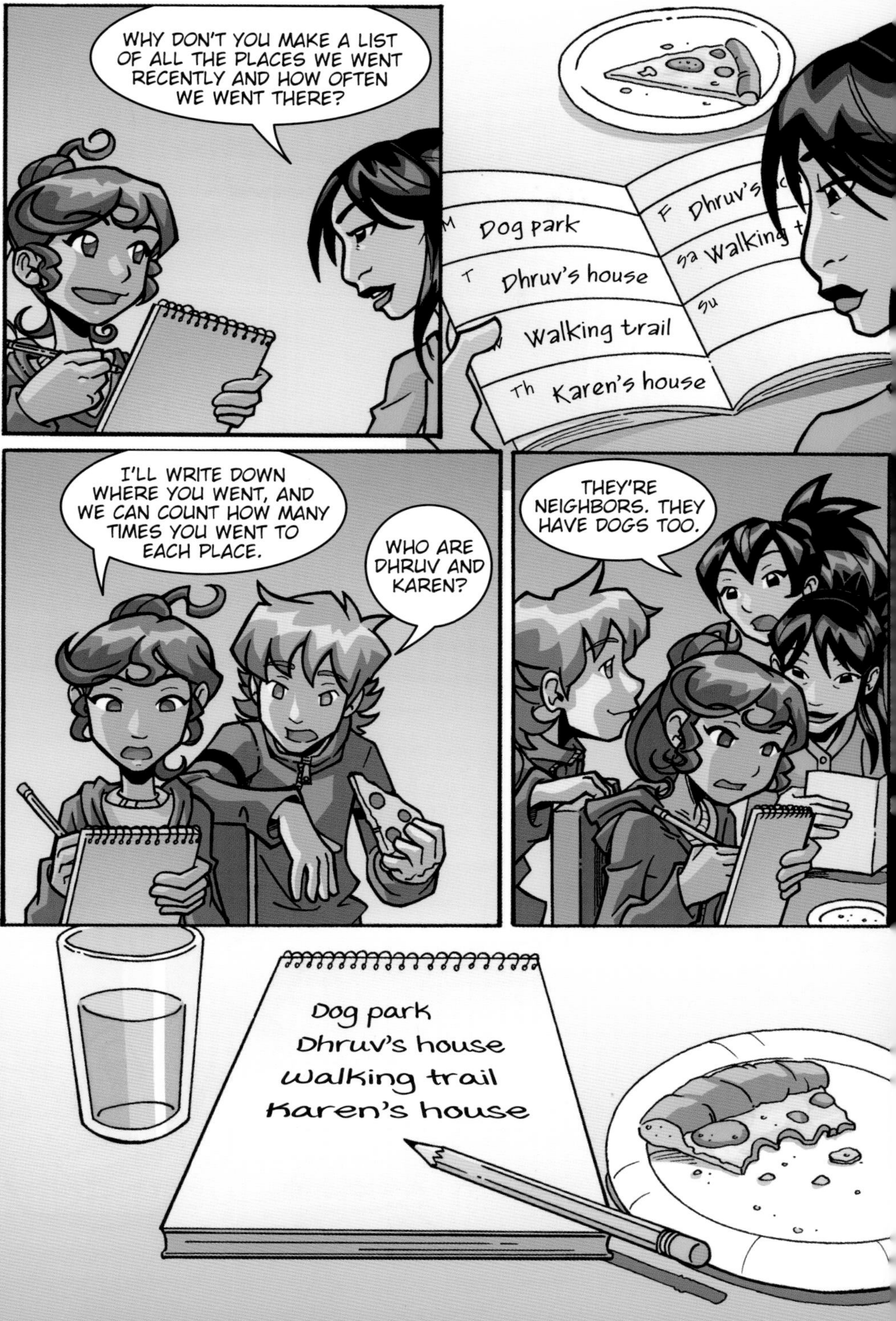
WHY DON'T YOU MAKE A LIST OF ALL THE PLACES WE WENT RECENTLY AND HOW OFTEN WE WENT THERE?
M Dog park
T Dhruv's house
Walking trail
Th Karen's house
F
Sa
Su
I'LL WRITE DOWN WHERE YOU WENT, AND WE CAN COUNT HOW MANY TIMES YOU WENT TO EACH PLACE.
WHO ARE DHRUV AND KAREN?
THEY'RE NEIGHBORS. THEY HAVE DOGS TOO.
Dog park
Dhruv's house
Walking trail
Karen's house

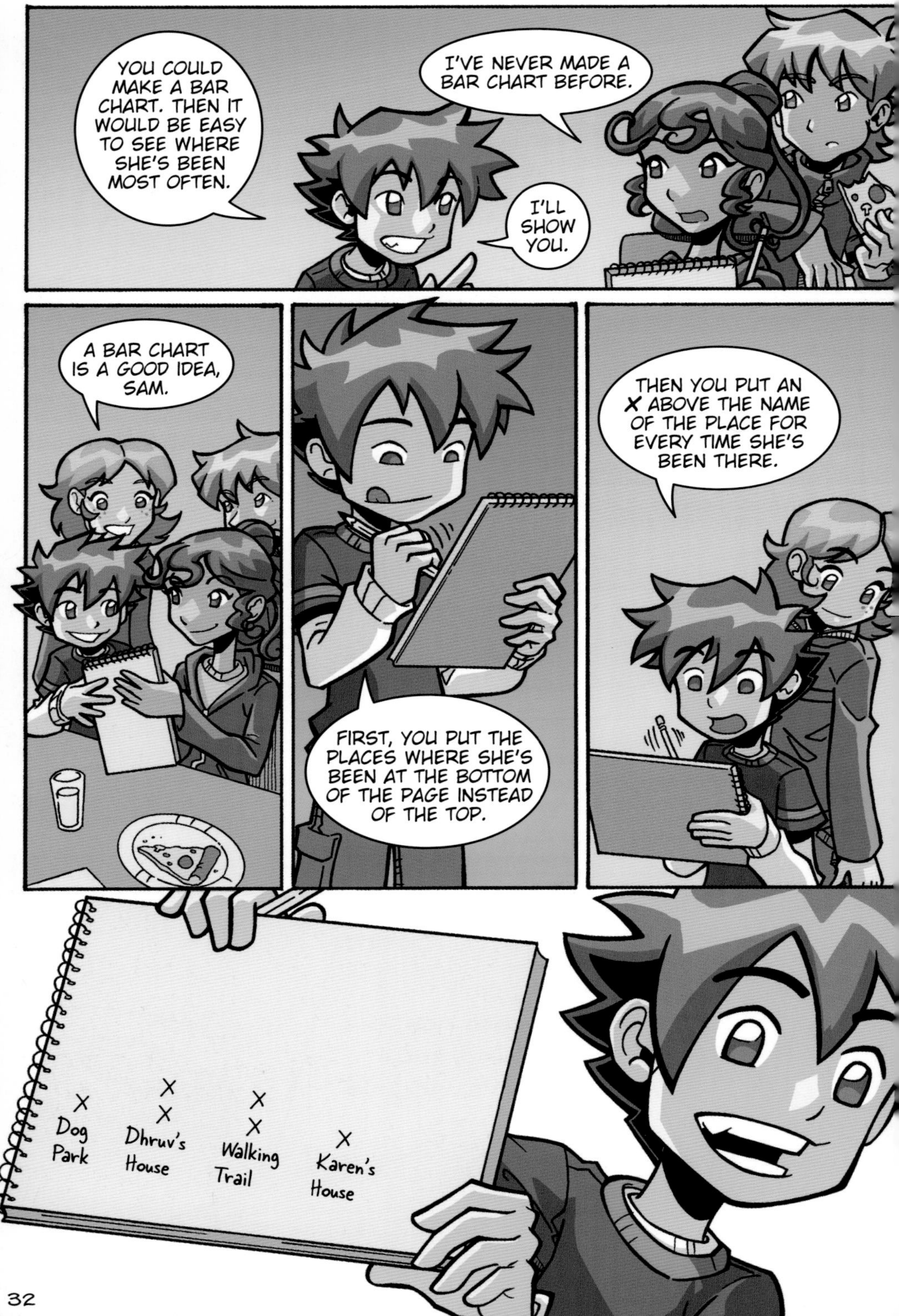
YOU COULD MAKE A BAR CHART. THEN IT WOULD BE EASY TO SEE WHERE SHE'S BEEN MOST OFTEN.
I'VE NEVER MADE A BAR CHART BEFORE.
I'LL SHOW YOU.
A BAR CHART IS A GOOD IDEA, SAM.
FIRST, YOU PUT THE PLACES WHERE SHE'S BEEN AT THE BOTTOM OF THE PAGE INSTEAD OF THE TOP.
THEN YOU PUT AN X ABOVE THE NAME OF THE PLACE FOR EVERY TIME SHE'S BEEN THERE.
X
Dog Park
X
X
Dhruv's House
X
X
Walking Trail
X
Karen's House

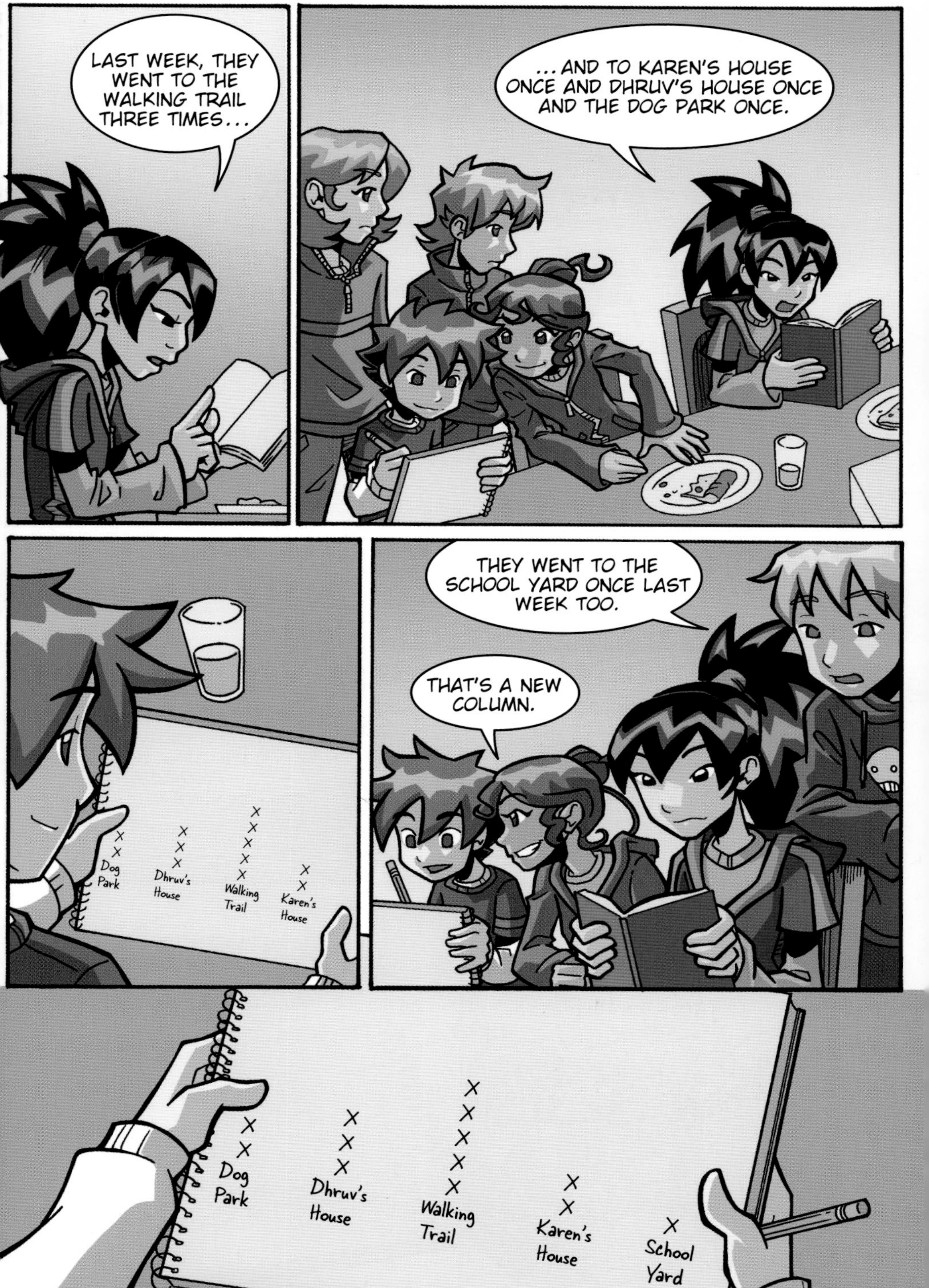
LAST WEEK, THEY WENT TO THE WALKING TRAIL THREE TIMES . . .
. . . AND TO KAREN'S HOUSE ONCE AND DHRUV'S HOUSE ONCE AND THE DOG PARK ONCE.
Dog Park
Dhruv's House
Walking Trail
Karen's House
THEY WENT TO THE SCHOOL YARD ONCE LAST WEEK TOO.
THAT'S A NEW COLUMN.
Dog Park
Dhruv's House
Walking Trail
Karen's House
School Yard

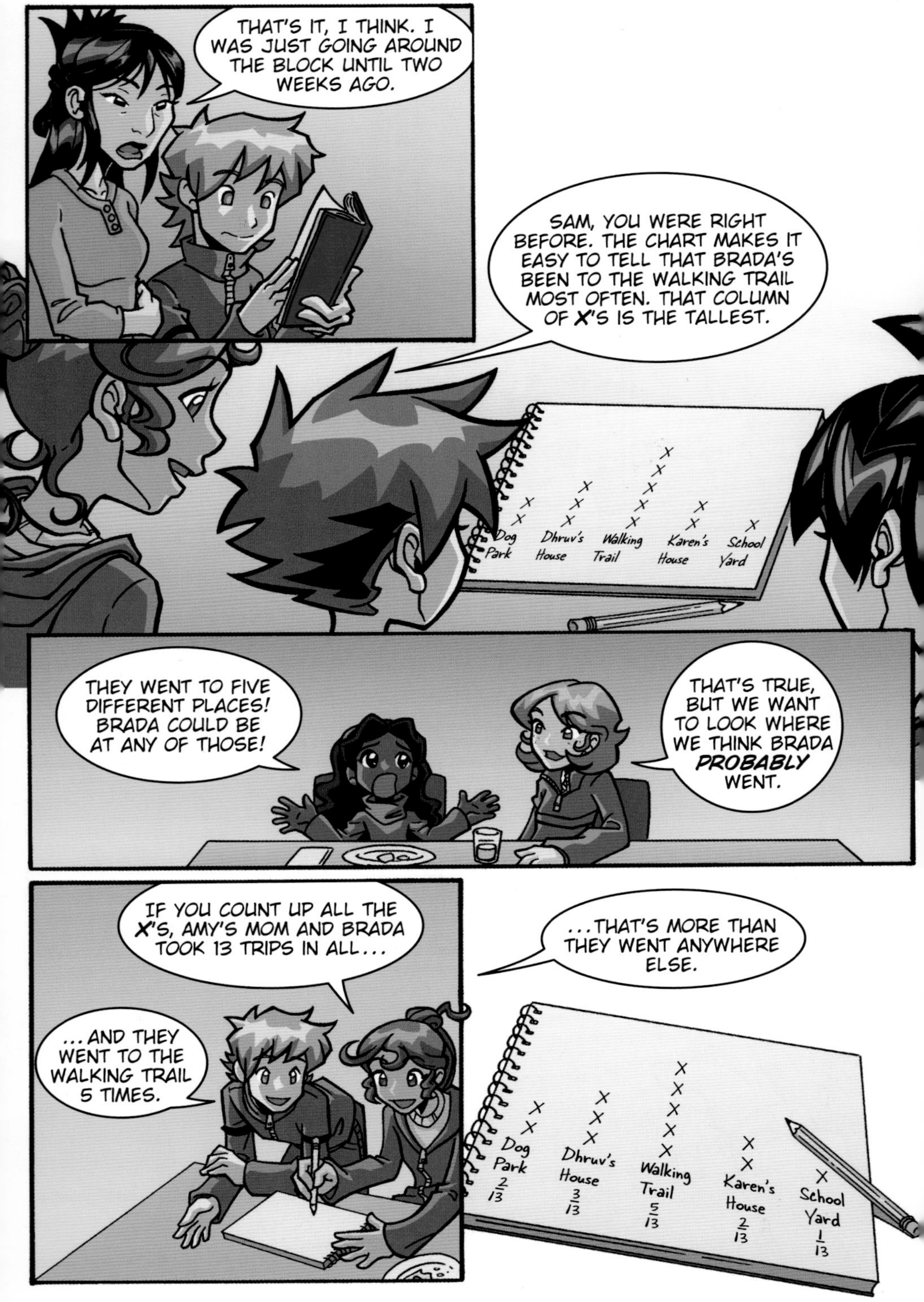
THAT'S IT, I THINK. I WAS JUST GOING AROUND THE BLOCK UNTIL TWO WEEKS AGO.
SAM, YOU WERE RIGHT BEFORE. THE CHART MAKES IT EASY TO TELL THAT BRADA'S BEEN TO THE WALKING TRAIL MOST OFTEN. THAT COLUMN OF X'S IS THE TALLEST.
Dog Park
Dhruv's House
Walking Trail
Karen's House
School Yard
THEY WENT TO FIVE DIFFERENT PLACES! BRADA COULD BE AT ANY OF THOSE!
THAT'S TRUE, BUT WE WANT TO LOOK WHERE WE THINK BRADA ***PROBABLY*** WENT.
IF YOU COUNT UP ALL THE X'S, AMY'S MOM AND BRADA TOOK 13 TRIPS IN ALL...
...AND THEY WENT TO THE WALKING TRAIL 5 TIMES.
...THAT'S MORE THAN THEY WENT ANYWHERE ELSE.
Dog Park 2/13
Dhruv's House 3/13
Walking Trail 5/13
Karen's House 2/13
School Yard 1/13

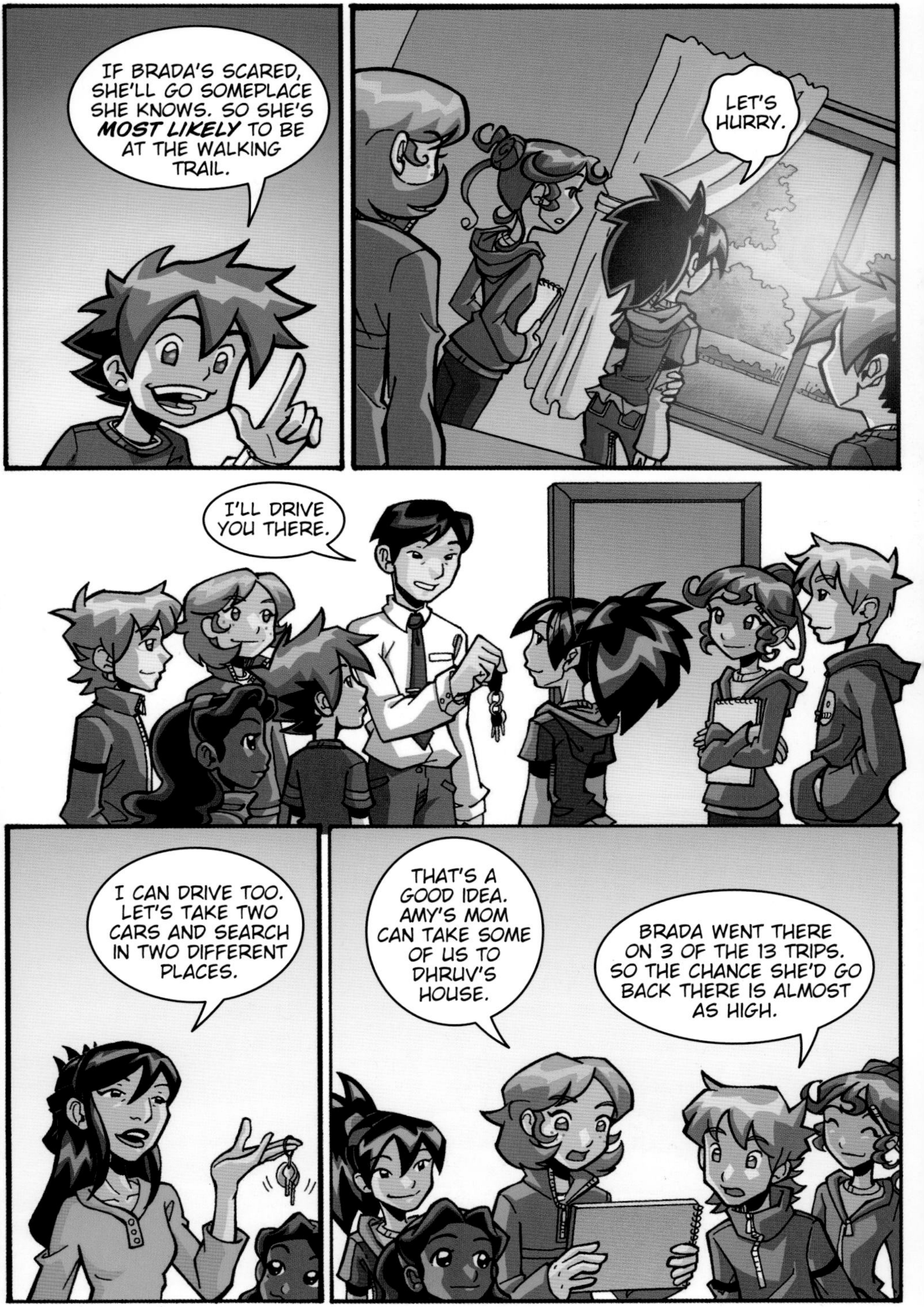
IF BRADA'S SCARED, SHE'LL GO SOMEPLACE SHE KNOWS. SO SHE'S MOST LIKELY TO BE AT THE WALKING TRAIL.
LET'S HURRY.
I'LL DRIVE YOU THERE.
I CAN DRIVE TOO. LET'S TAKE TWO CARS AND SEARCH IN TWO DIFFERENT PLACES.
THAT'S A GOOD IDEA. AMY'S MOM CAN TAKE SOME OF US TO DHRUV'S HOUSE.
BRADA WENT THERE ON 3 OF THE 13 TRIPS. SO THE CHANCE SHE'D GO BACK THERE IS ALMOST AS HIGH.

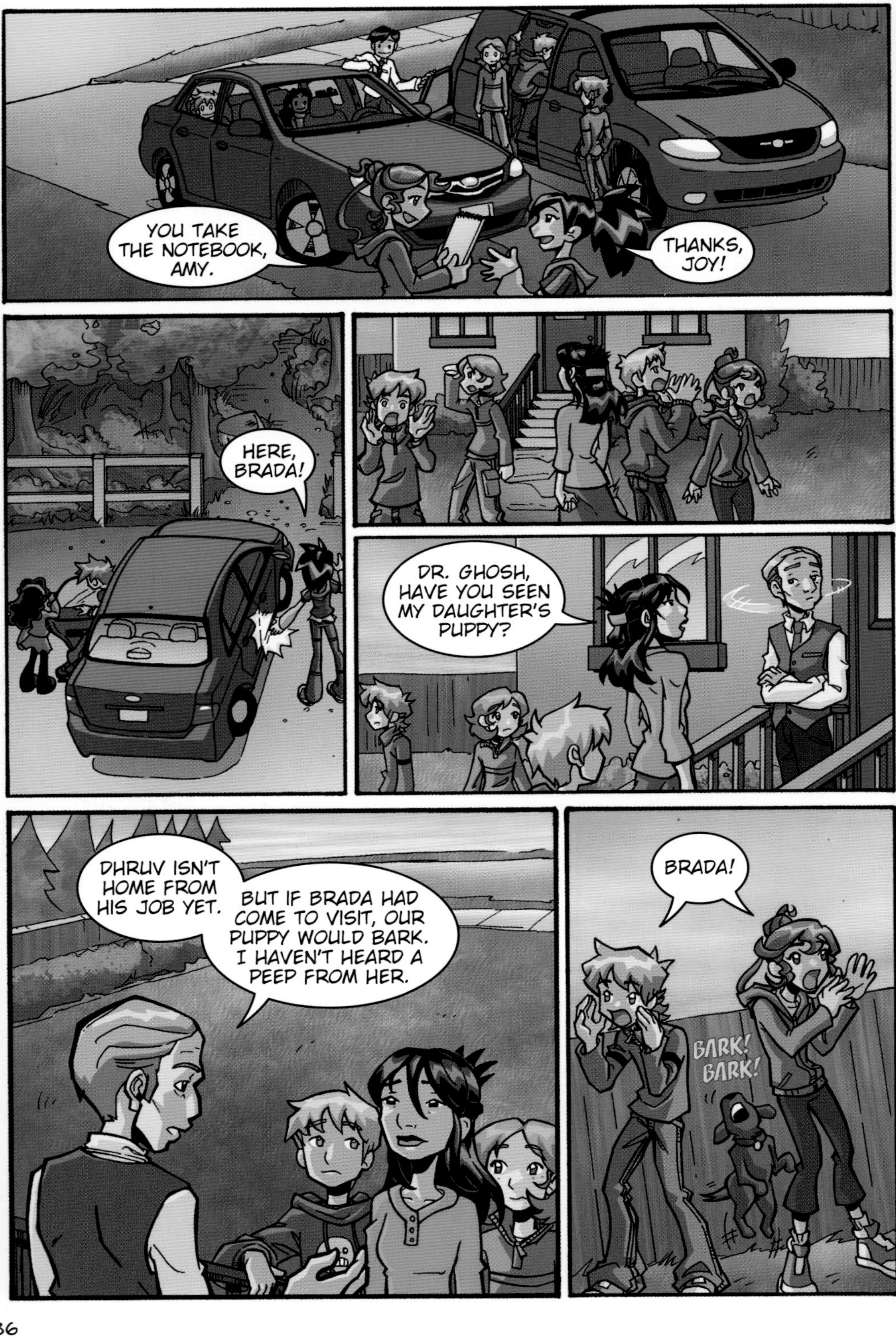
YOU TAKE THE NOTEBOOK, AMY.
THANKS, JOY!
HERE, BRADA!
DR. GHOSH, HAVE YOU SEEN MY DAUGHTER'S PUPPY?
DHRUV ISN'T HOME FROM HIS JOB YET.
BUT IF BRADA HAD COME TO VISIT, OUR PUPPY WOULD BARK. I HAVEN'T HEARD A PEEP FROM HER.
BRADA!
BARK! BARK!

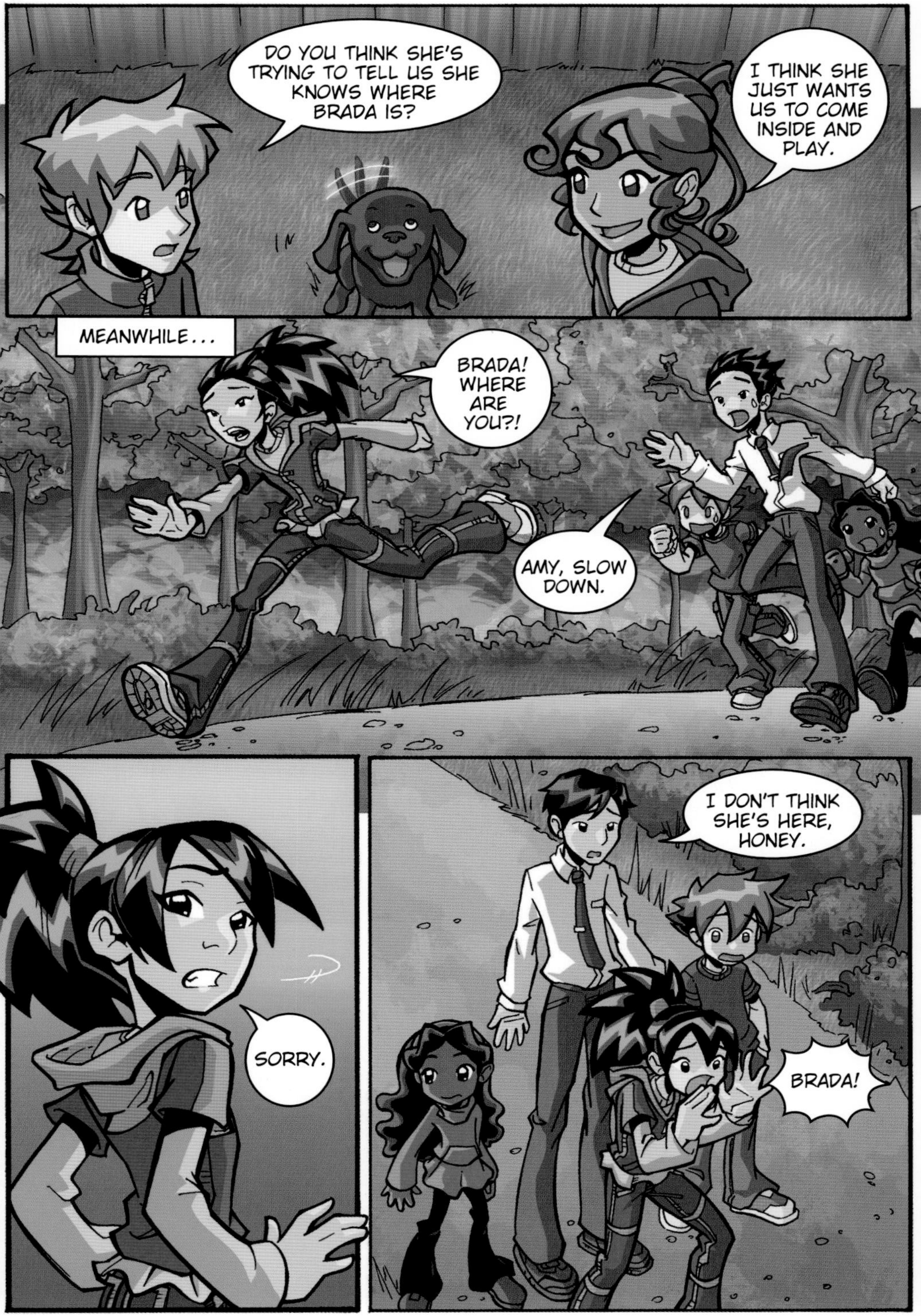
DO YOU THINK SHE'S TRYING TO TELL US SHE KNOWS WHERE BRADA IS?
I THINK SHE JUST WANTS US TO COME INSIDE AND PLAY.
MEANWHILE...
BRADA! WHERE ARE YOU?!
AMY, SLOW DOWN.
SORRY.
I DON'T THINK SHE'S HERE, HONEY.
BRADA!

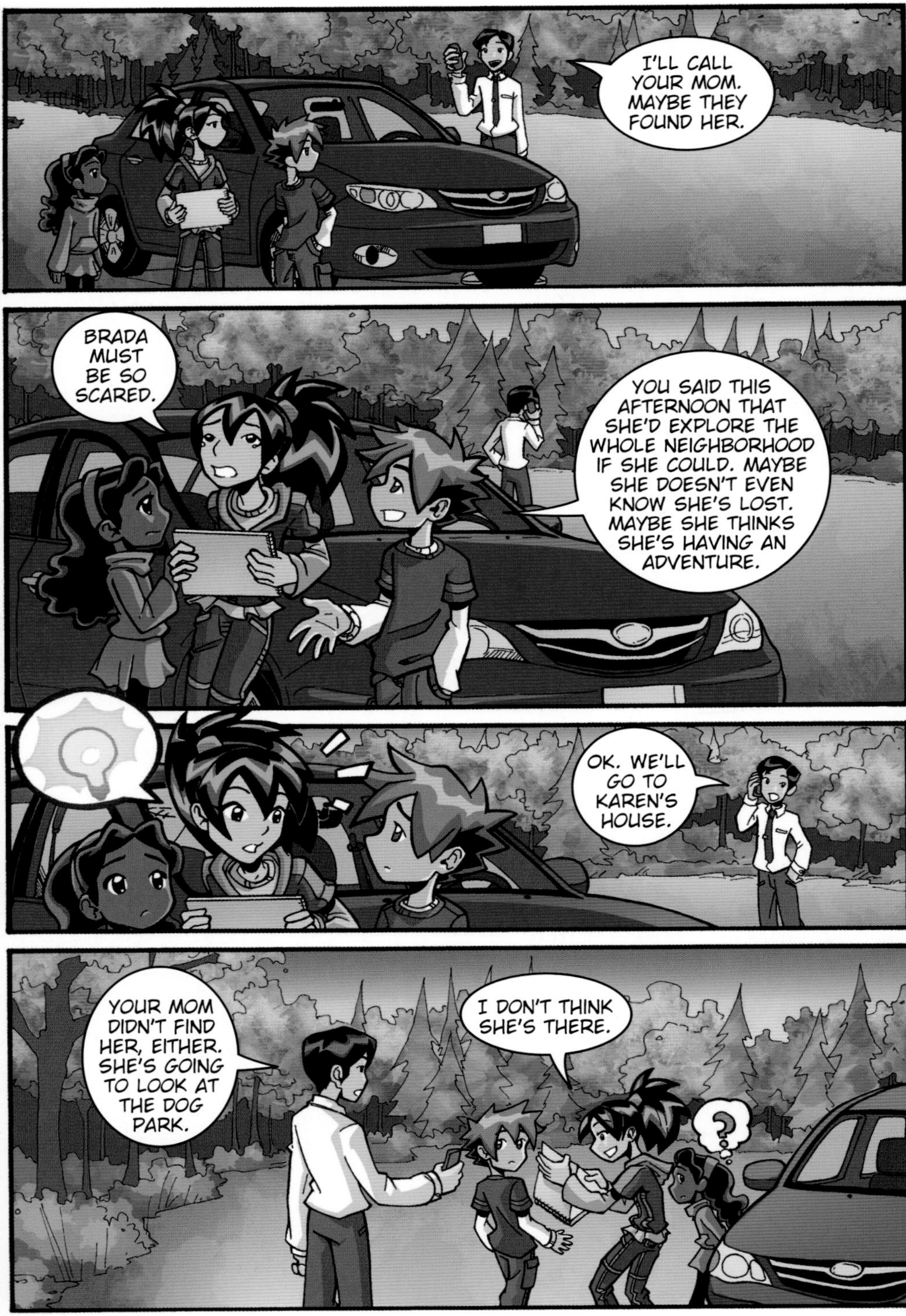
I'LL CALL YOUR MOM. MAYBE THEY FOUND HER.
BRADA MUST BE SO SCARED.
YOU SAID THIS AFTERNOON THAT SHE'D EXPLORE THE WHOLE NEIGHBORHOOD IF SHE COULD. MAYBE SHE DOESN'T EVEN KNOW SHE'S LOST. MAYBE SHE THINKS SHE'S HAVING AN ADVENTURE.
OK. WE'LL GO TO KAREN'S HOUSE.
YOUR MOM DIDN'T FIND HER, EITHER. SHE'S GOING TO LOOK AT THE DOG PARK.
I DON'T THINK SHE'S THERE.

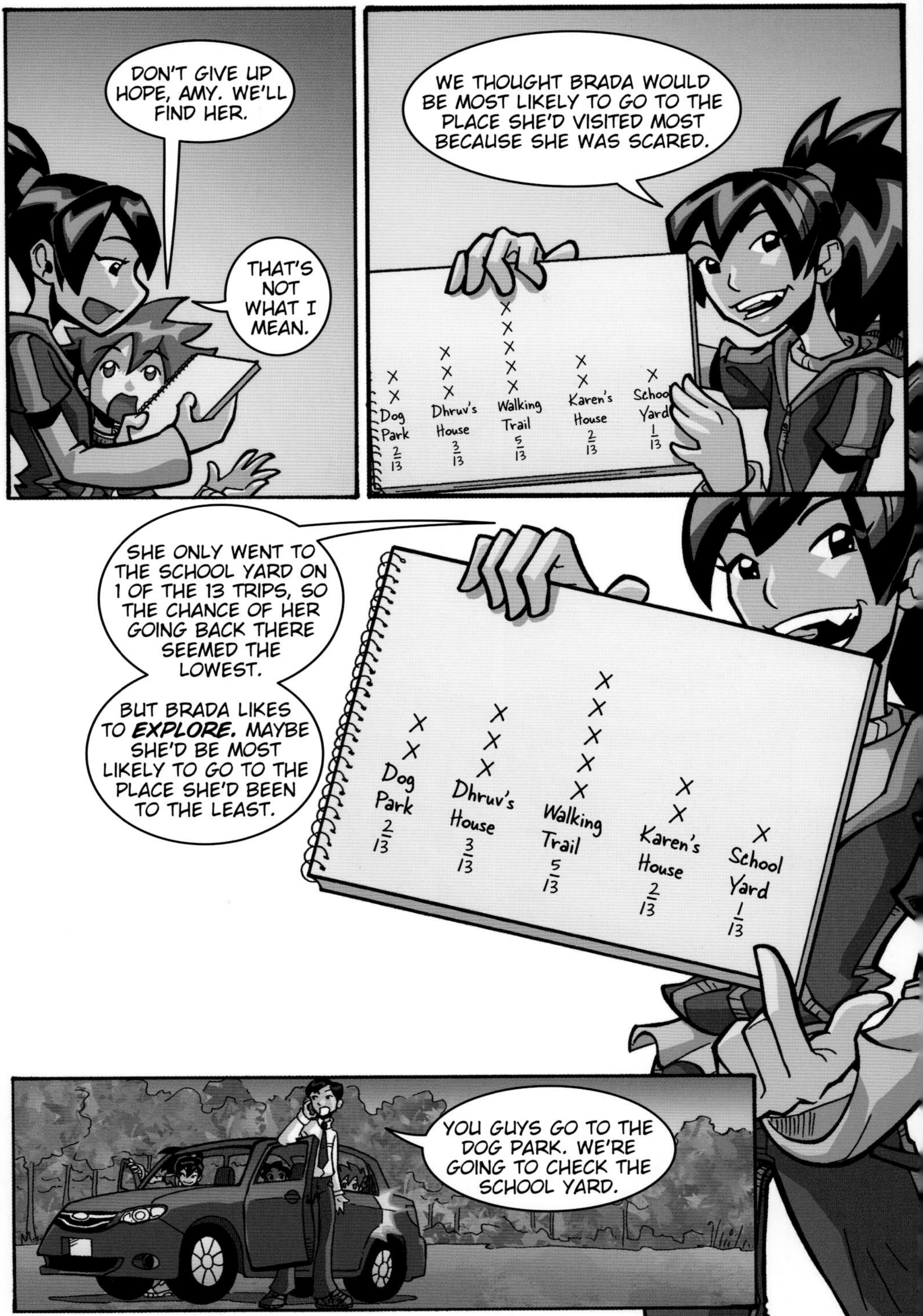
DON'T GIVE UP HOPE, AMY. WE'LL FIND HER.
THAT'S NOT WHAT I MEAN.
WE THOUGHT BRADA WOULD BE MOST LIKELY TO GO TO THE PLACE SHE'D VISITED MOST BECAUSE SHE WAS SCARED.
Dog Park 2/13
Dhruv's House 3/13
Walking Trail 5/13
Karen's House 2/13
School Yard 1/13
SHE ONLY WENT TO THE SCHOOL YARD ON 1 OF THE 13 TRIPS, SO THE CHANCE OF HER GOING BACK THERE SEEMED THE LOWEST.
BUT BRADA LIKES TO ***EXPLORE.*** MAYBE SHE'D BE MOST LIKELY TO GO TO THE PLACE SHE'D BEEN TO THE LEAST.
Dog Park 2/13
Dhruv's House 3/13
Walking Trail 5/13
Karen's House 2/13
School Yard 1/13
YOU GUYS GO TO THE DOG PARK. WE'RE GOING TO CHECK THE SCHOOL YARD.

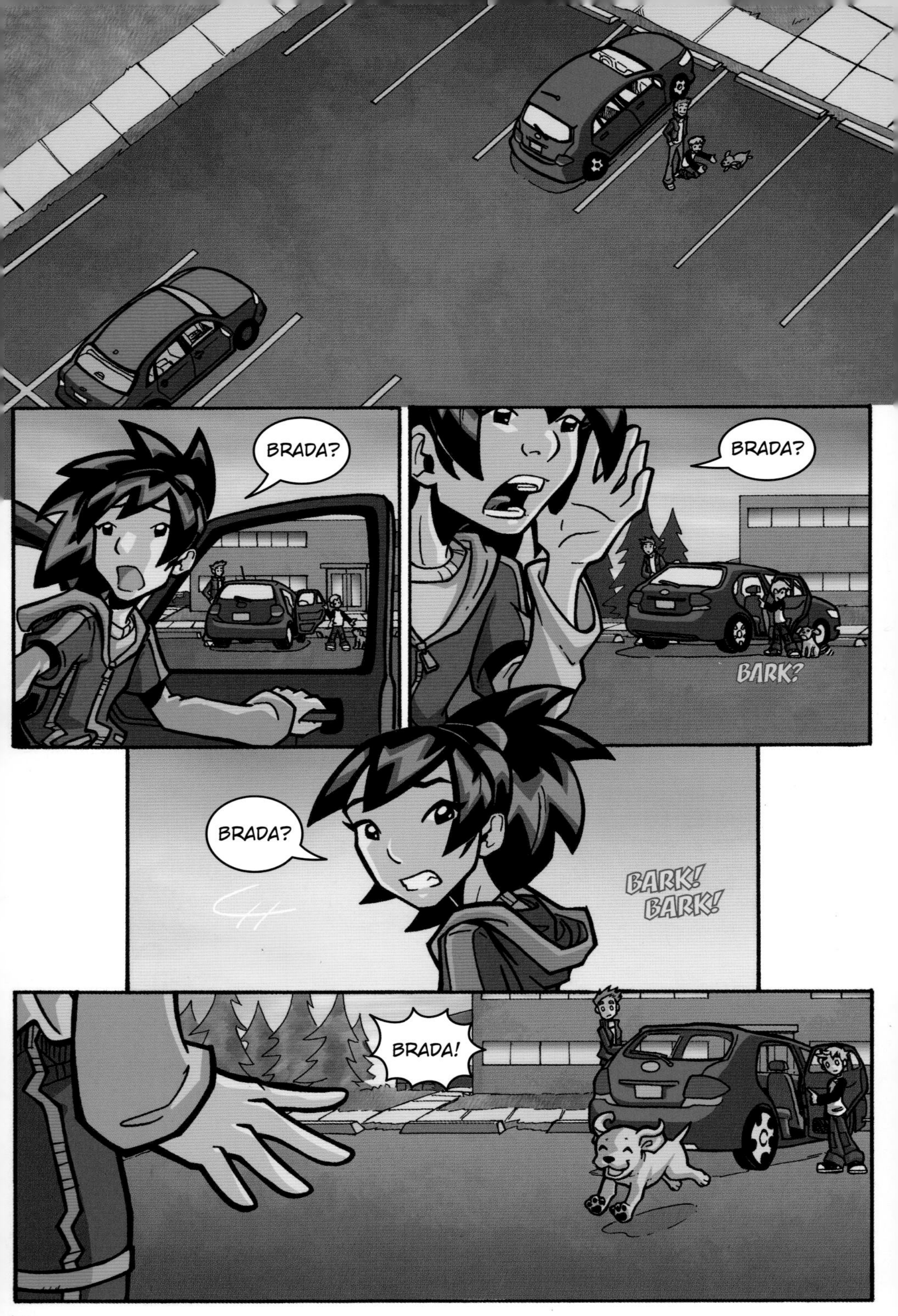
BRADA?
BRADA?
BARK?
BRADA?
BARK! BARK!
BRADA!

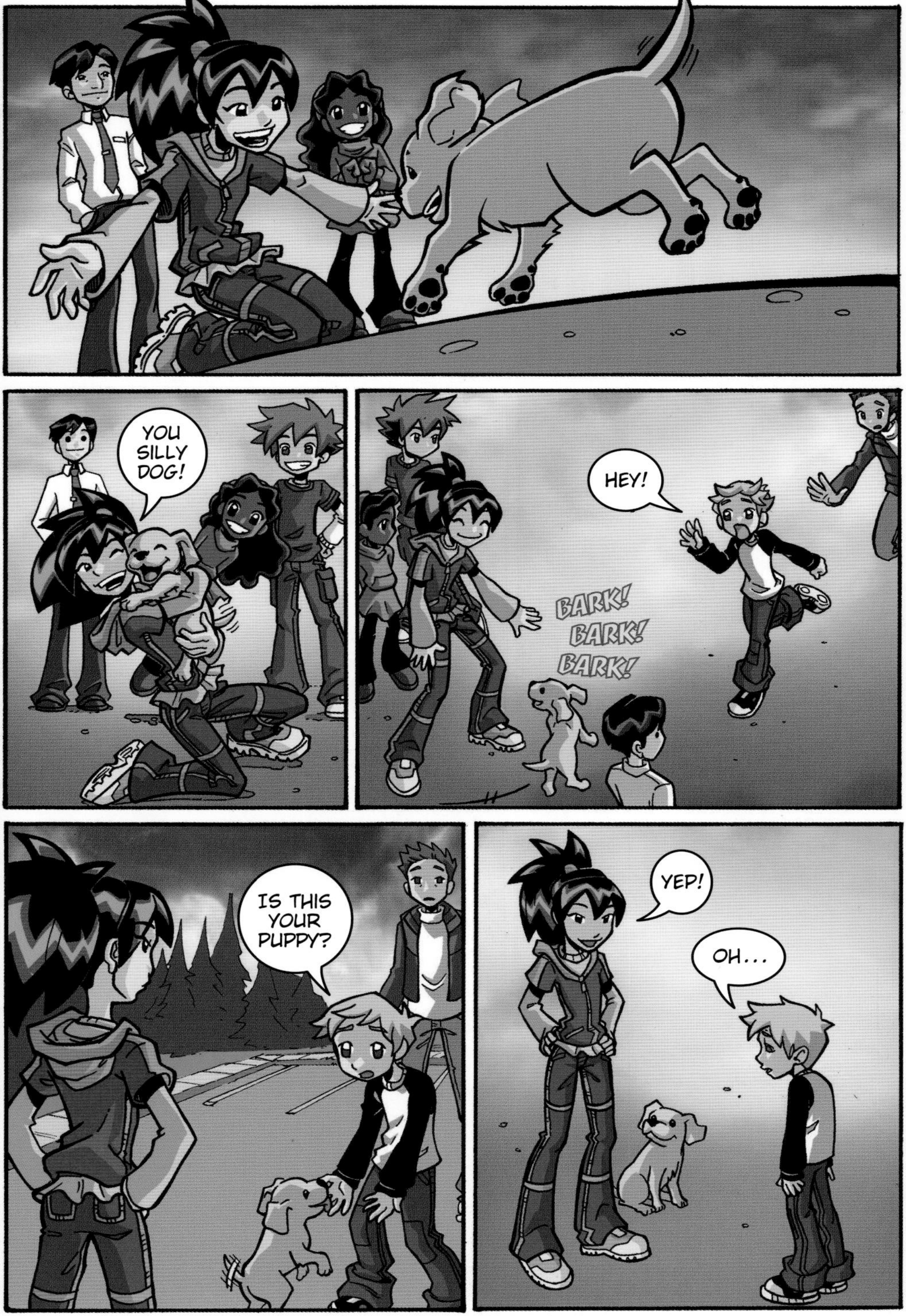
YOU SILLY DOG!
HEY!
BARK! BARK! BARK!
IS THIS YOUR PUPPY?
YEP!
OH...

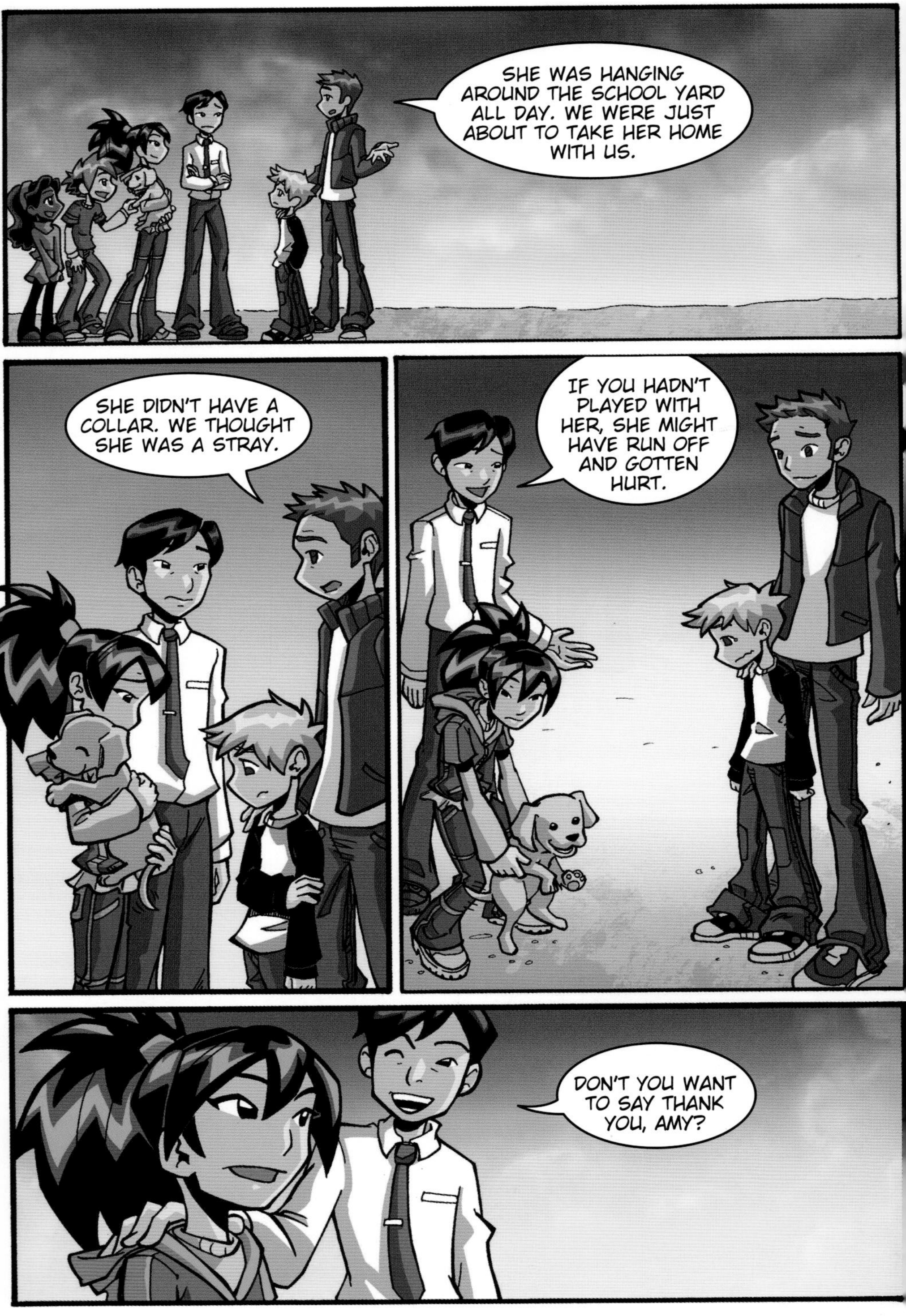
SHE WAS HANGING AROUND THE SCHOOL YARD ALL DAY. WE WERE JUST ABOUT TO TAKE HER HOME WITH US.
SHE DIDN'T HAVE A COLLAR. WE THOUGHT SHE WAS A STRAY.
IF YOU HADN'T PLAYED WITH HER, SHE MIGHT HAVE RUN OFF AND GOTTEN HURT.
DON'T YOU WANT TO SAY THANK YOU, AMY?

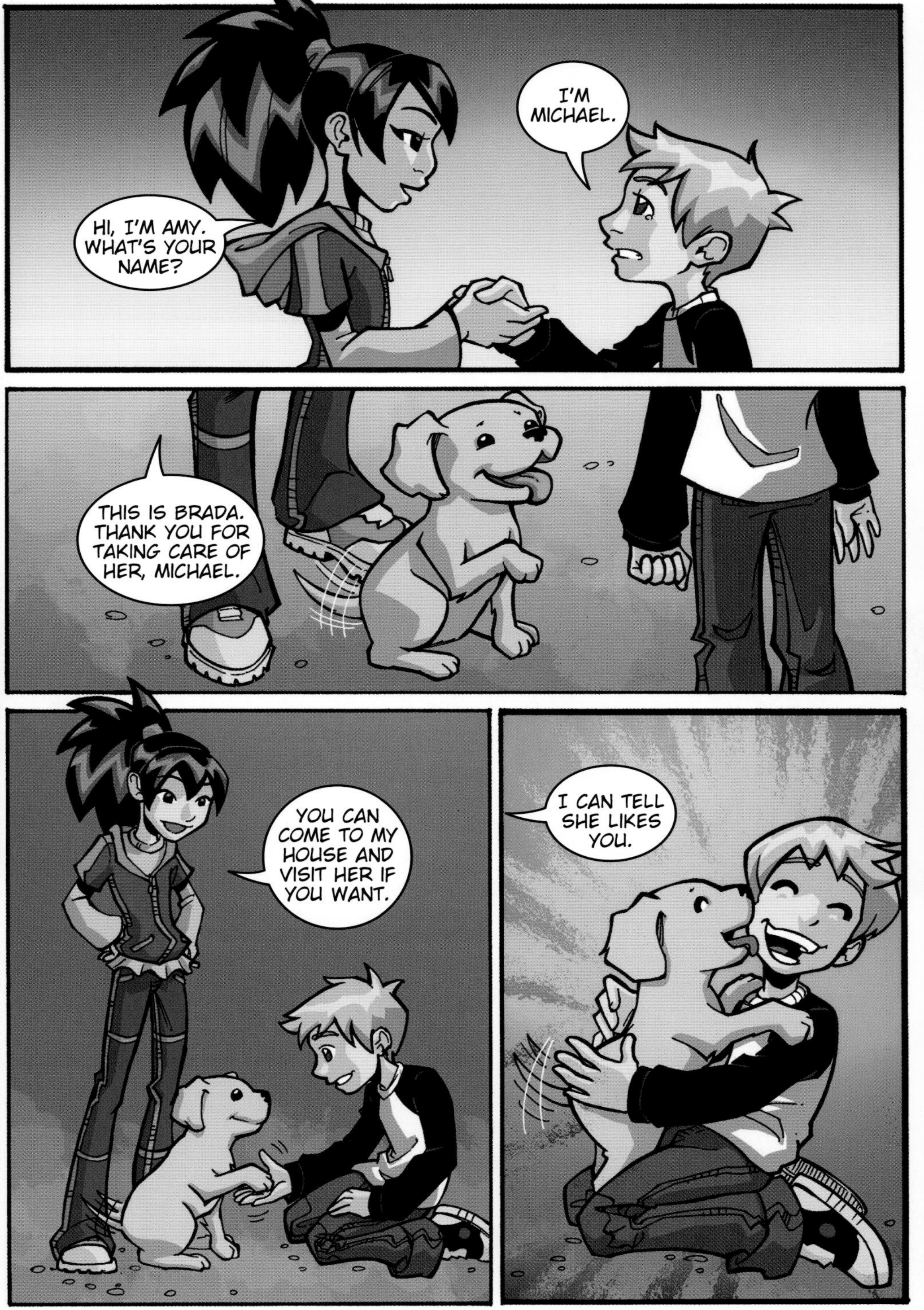
HI, I'M AMY. WHAT'S YOUR NAME?
I'M MICHAEL.
THIS IS BRADA. THANK YOU FOR TAKING CARE OF HER, MICHAEL.
YOU CAN COME TO MY HOUSE AND VISIT HER IF YOU WANT.
I CAN TELL SHE LIKES YOU.

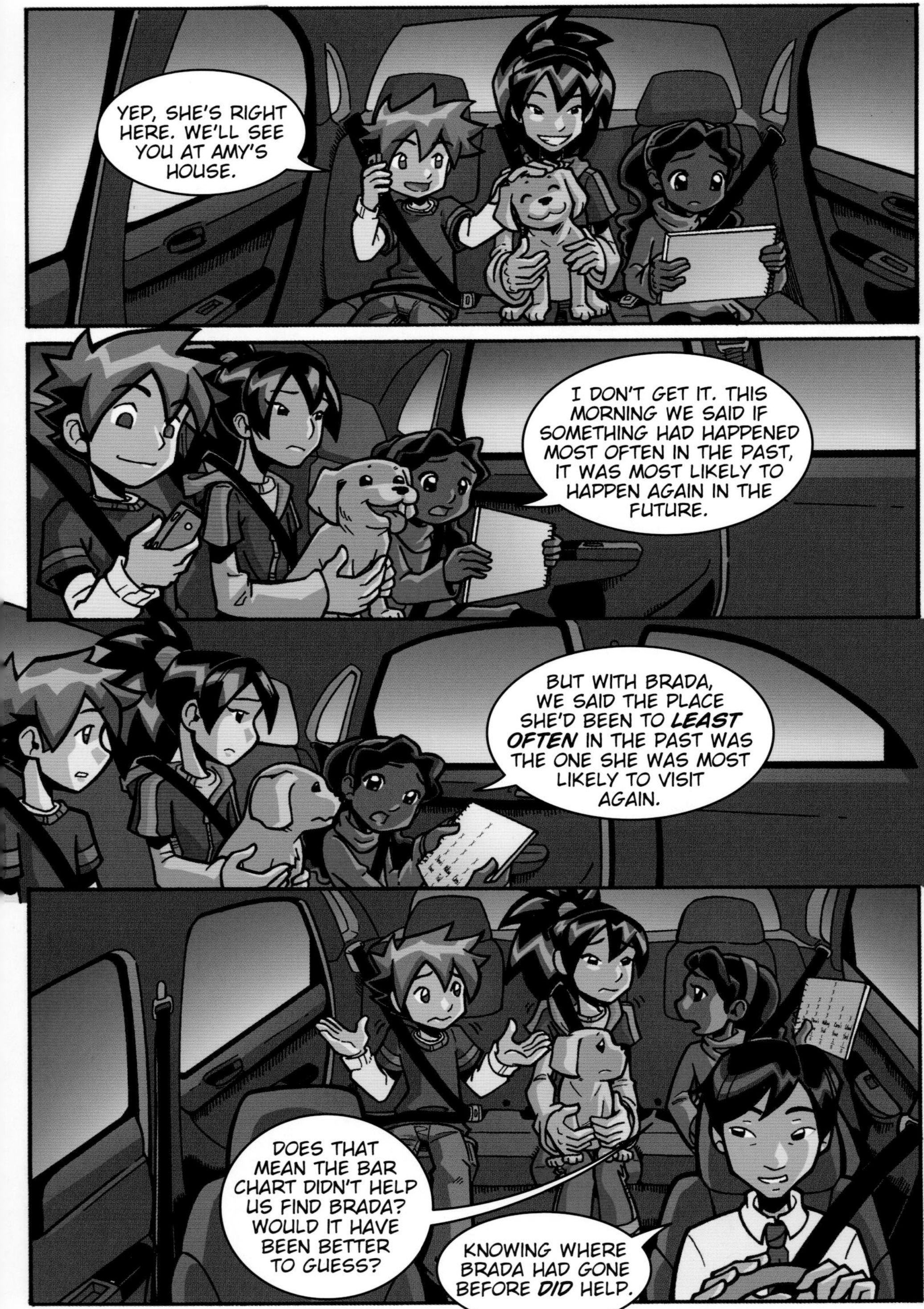
YEP, SHE'S RIGHT HERE. WE'LL SEE YOU AT AMY'S HOUSE.
I DON'T GET IT. THIS MORNING WE SAID IF SOMETHING HAD HAPPENED MOST OFTEN IN THE PAST, IT WAS MOST LIKELY TO HAPPEN AGAIN IN THE FUTURE.
BUT WITH BRADA, WE SAID THE PLACE SHE'D BEEN TO ***LEAST OFTEN*** IN THE PAST WAS THE ONE SHE WAS MOST LIKELY TO VISIT AGAIN.
DOES THAT MEAN THE BAR CHART DIDN'T HELP US FIND BRADA? WOULD IT HAVE BEEN BETTER TO GUESS?
KNOWING WHERE BRADA HAD GONE BEFORE ***DID*** HELP.

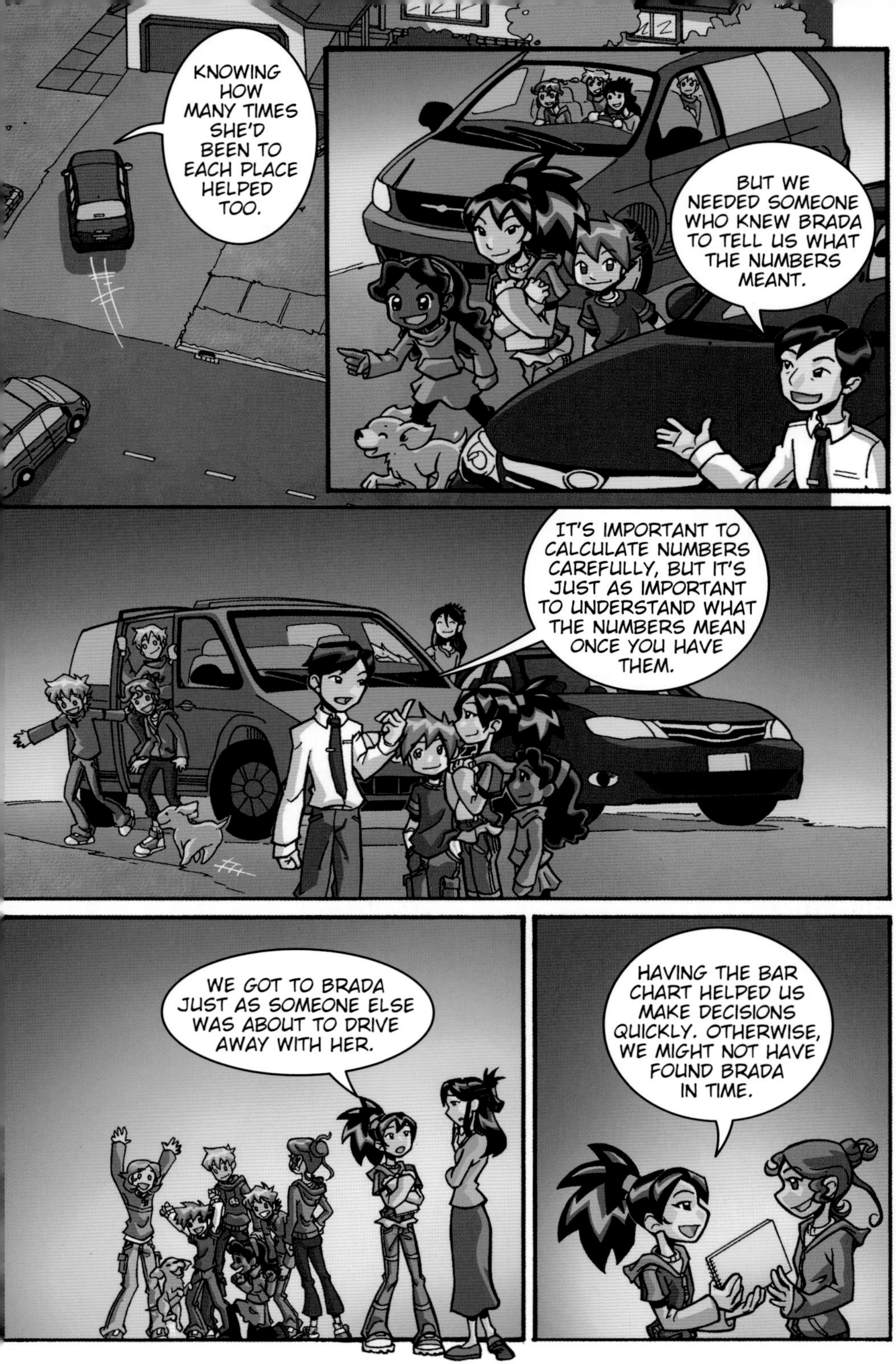
KNOWING HOW MANY TIMES SHE'D BEEN TO EACH PLACE HELPED TOO.
BUT WE NEEDED SOMEONE WHO KNEW BRADA TO TELL US WHAT THE NUMBERS MEANT.
IT'S IMPORTANT TO CALCULATE NUMBERS CAREFULLY, BUT IT'S JUST AS IMPORTANT TO UNDERSTAND WHAT THE NUMBERS MEAN ONCE YOU HAVE THEM.
WE GOT TO BRADA JUST AS SOMEONE ELSE WAS ABOUT TO DRIVE AWAY WITH HER.
HAVING THE BAR CHART HELPED US MAKE DECISIONS QUICKLY. OTHERWISE, WE MIGHT NOT HAVE FOUND BRADA IN TIME.

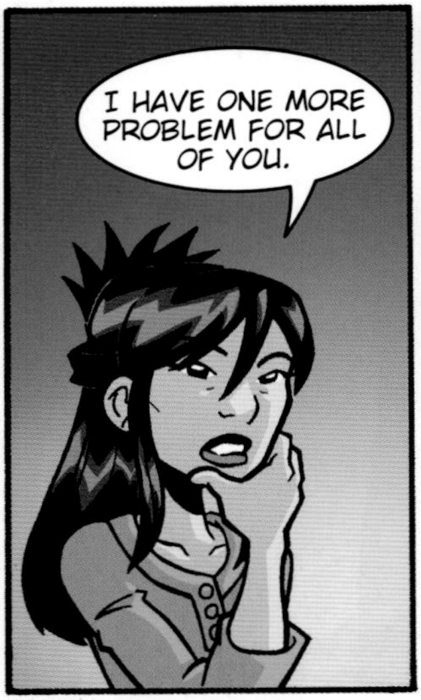
I HAVE ONE MORE PROBLEM FOR ALL OF YOU.

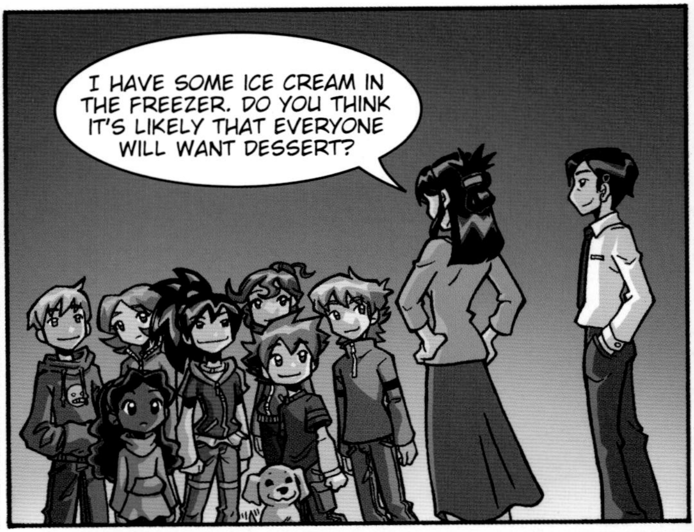
I HAVE SOME ICE CREAM IN THE FREEZER. DO YOU THINK IT'S LIKELY THAT EVERYONE WILL WANT DESSERT?

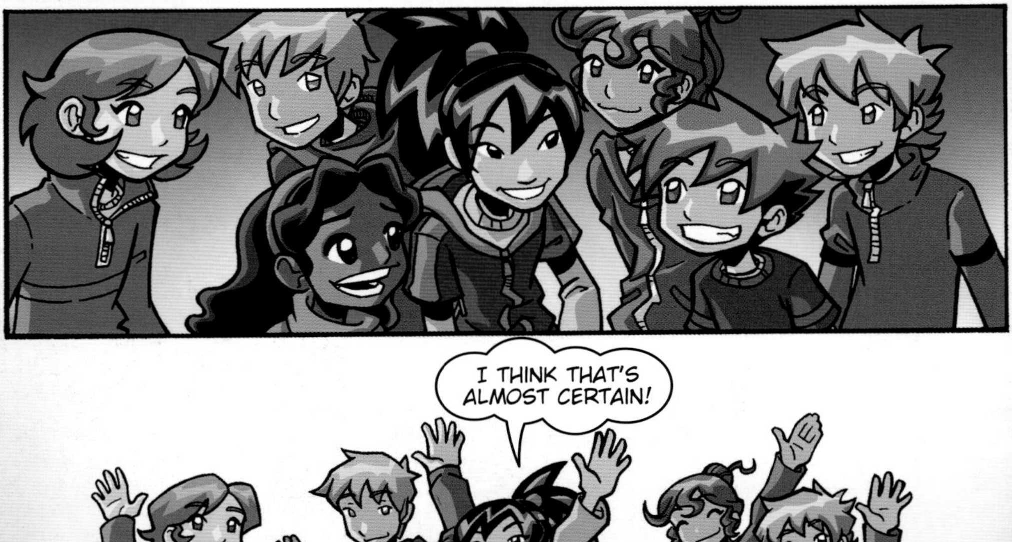

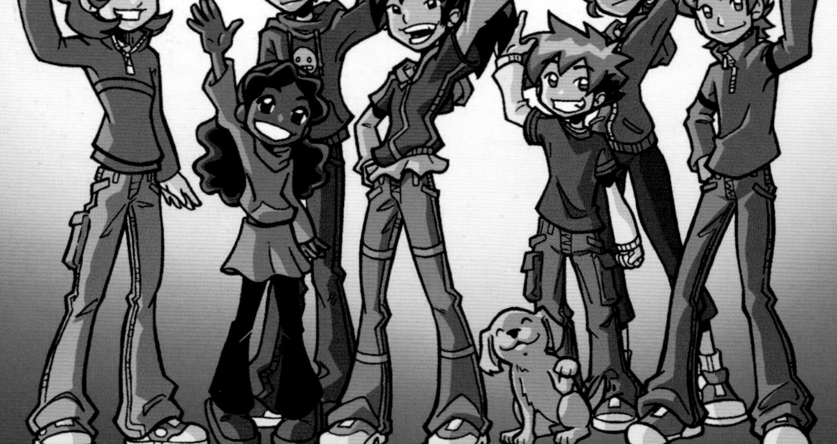
I THINK THAT'S ALMOST CERTAIN!

The Authors

Melinda Thielbar is a teacher who has written math courses for all ages, from kids to adults. In 2005 Melinda was awarded a VIGRE fellowship at North Carolina State University for PhD candidates "likely to make a strong contribution to education in mathematics." She lives in Raleigh, North Carolina, with her husband, author and video game programmer Richard Dansky, and their two cats.

Lydia Barriman is a teacher, doctoral candidate, and writer of math courses for all ages.

The Artists

Tintin Pantoja was born in Manila in the Philippines. She received a degree in Illustration and Cartooning from the School of Visual Arts (SVA) in New York City and was nominated for the Friends of Lulu "Best Newcomer" award. She was also a finalist in Tokyopop's Rising Stars of Manga 5.

Yali Lin was born in southern China and lived there for 11 years before moving to New York and graduating from SVA. She loves climbing trees, walking barefoot on grass, and chasing dragonflies. When not drawing, she teaches cartooning to teens.

Becky Grutzik received a degree in illustration from the University of Wisconsin-Stevens Point. In her free time, she and her husband, Matt Wendt, teach a class to kids on how to draw manga and superheroes.

Jenn Manley Lee was born in Clovis, New Mexico. After many travels, she settled in Portland, Oregon, where she works as a graphic designer. She keeps the home she shares with spouse Kip Manley and daughter Taran full of books, geeks, art, cats, and music.

Candice Chow studied animation at SVA and followed her interests through comics, manga, and graphic design. Her previous books include *Macbeth* (Wiley) with fellow SVA graduate **Eve Grandt**, who lives and works in Brooklyn, New York.

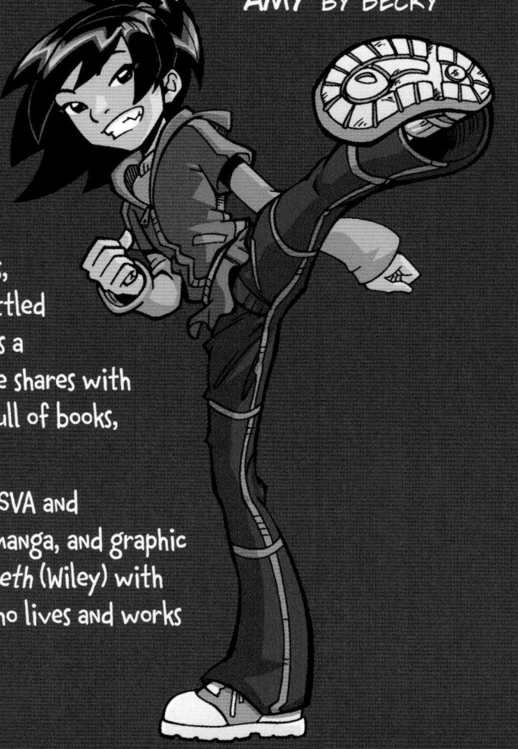

AMY BY BECKY

JOIN THE KIDS FROM THE KUNG FU SCHOOL IN SOLVING ALL THE MANGA MATH MYSTERIES

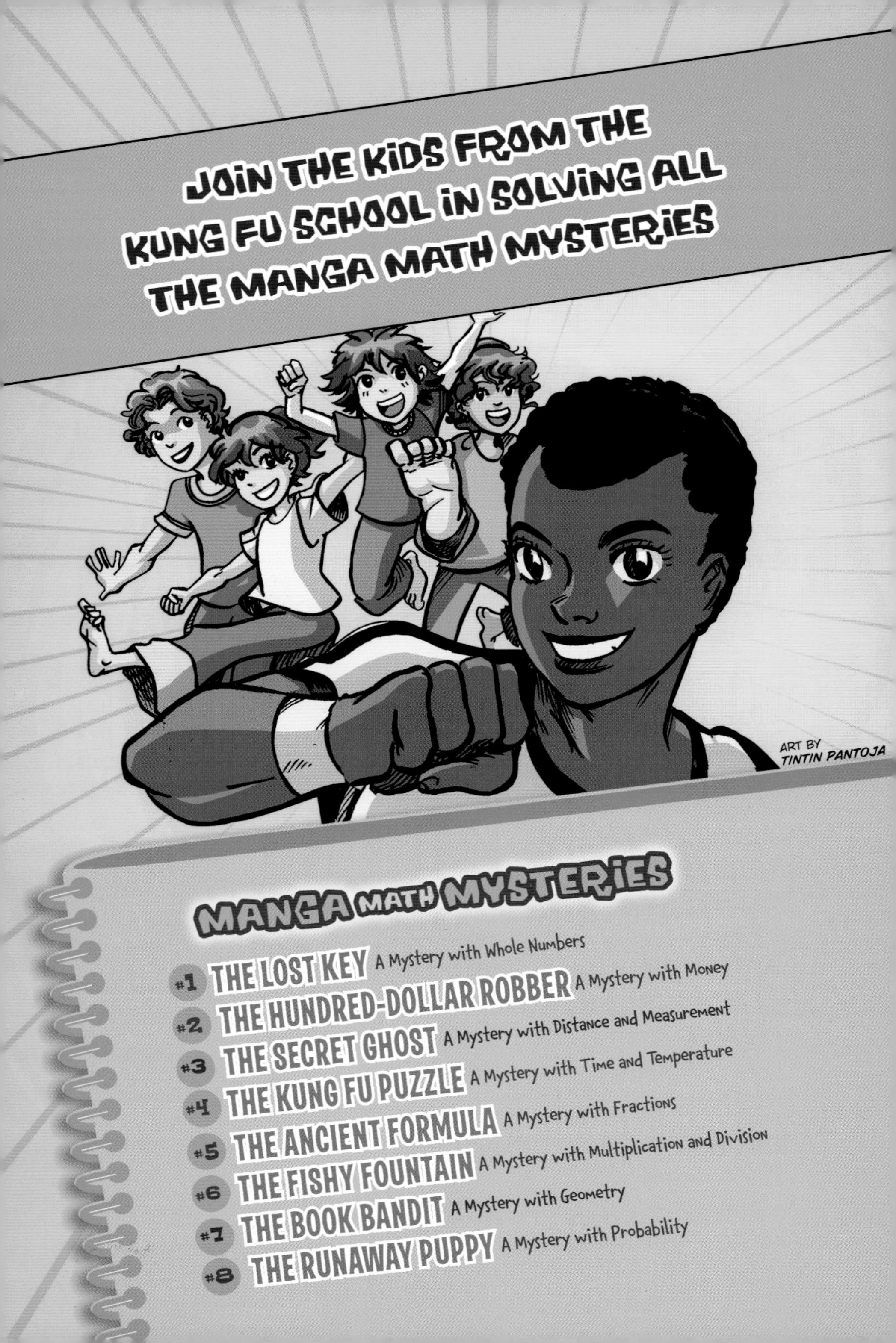
ART BY
TINTIN PANTOJA

MANGA MATH MYSTERIES

- #1 **THE LOST KEY** A Mystery with Whole Numbers
- #2 **THE HUNDRED-DOLLAR ROBBER** A Mystery with Money
- #3 **THE SECRET GHOST** A Mystery with Distance and Measurement
- #4 **THE KUNG FU PUZZLE** A Mystery with Time and Temperature
- #5 **THE ANCIENT FORMULA** A Mystery with Fractions
- #6 **THE FISHY FOUNTAIN** A Mystery with Multiplication and Division
- #7 **THE BOOK BANDIT** A Mystery with Geometry
- #8 **THE RUNAWAY PUPPY** A Mystery with Probability